AMBUSH!

There were a good two dozen heavily armed men down the slope below Gringo lying in wait for the Red Cross expedition. They had chosen pretty good cover behind rocks and bushes.

He wasn't quite sure why he did it, but he grabbed his Maxim, armed it, and turned to move down the slope just as the bandits opened fire.

The first thing the bandits hit was the poor khaki-clad sucker leading the first supply mule. Another Red Cross worker folded like a jackknife to hit the dust beside him while the rest of the column scattered in every direction, abandoning their supply mules just as they were supposed to.

It was a swell little ambush...until Captain Gringo opened up with the machine gun!

Novels by
Ramsay Thorne

Published by
WARNER BOOKS

Renegade #23

VOLCANO OF VIOLENCE

Ramsay Thorne

WARNER BOOKS

A Warner Communications Company

Renegade #23

VOLCANO OF VIOLENCE

The three thugs who saved Captain Gringo's neck that night in Punta Carreta were hardly out to do him any favors as he slugged it out with them in a dark alley near the waterfront.

He'd been on his way back to the schooner when he'd been jumped by the usual three-man team in a fairly professional manner. Their basic mistake had been the assumption that two of them were about to pin the big soldier of fortune's arms and hold him long enough for the third thug to pat him down for goodies.

He'd proven them wrong by throwing the first one who'd grabbed him over his shoulder, kicking the next in the nuts, and putting the third on the ground with a nice right cross. But then, as he'd tried simply to leave it at that and walk away, the dumb sons of bitches had gotten back up and come to him again. So by now it was starting to look like they really wanted a serious argument.

The tall blond American was in pretty good shape to offer them one. He was packing a double-action .38 in the shoulder rig hidden under his linen jacket. But he didn't want to draw attention to his presence in Punta Carreta if it could be avoided. A knock-around guy with a price on his head and no understanding with the local law could attract more attention than he really wanted to by shooting up the local citizenry.

As the one he'd decked with the right cross moved into range, the big Yank proved how some guys never learn, by dropping him again with the same punch. But, before he could stomp the idiot, another bored in, windmilling, and had to be stopped with a left hook. It stopped him pretty good. So now there was only one left on his feet, and if he'd had any sense he would have been scampering off by now. He was the smallest of the three.

The remaining thug didn't like the odds, either. So he whipped out a six-inch blade to give himself a literal edge as he dropped into a knife fighter's crouch, slowly waving the blade from side to side, as if he thought he was an alley cat and the knife was his tail or something.

Captain Gringo shook his head wearily and said, "You'd better put that thing away before one of us gets hurt, muchacho. I'm not carrying enough dinero to justify a killing."

The knife fighter minced closer as he purred, "I do not wish for to cut you for your money now, Yanqui. There is a saying in my village. When the tree refuses for to bend for the wind, one must cut it down!"

"Hey, that's really neat. Did you ever hear what the Mexicans say about the open mouth attracting flies?"

The ladino didn't answer as he braced himself for the final rush.

Captain Gringo braced himself, too. Like most knock-around guys, the big American had learned by now, the hard way, that a man seriously intent on stabbing someone seldom waved the blade about for inspection or announced his intentions in advance. On the other hand, none of these guys was acting too sensible this evening and there was always the chance of meeting a jerk-off who didn't know the rules of the game.

In the dim light, Captain Gringo tried to read the other man's eyes. He could just make them out. The knife waver's face was blank. But his alley-cat eyes betrayed expectancy, as if he was waiting for something to happen before he made his move. So Captain Gringo didn't move. A tense million years went by. Then a familiar voice behind Captain Gringo snapped, "Dick! *Hit* it!"

So Captain Gringo dove for the dirt, just in time, as another knife spun end over end through the space his back had just filled.

The thug he'd been facing didn't move fast enough. He caught the thrown blade to the hilt with his chest, gasped, dropped his own knife, and followed it down!

Captain Gringo rolled over, drawing his own .38 as he growled, "Enough of this shit." But then he saw he didn't need his less-silent weapon after all and put it away. He rose to his feet, nodding, as he said, "Thanks. Last time I counted, there were three of the pricks. I only see two now."

Gaston Verrier finished wiping his own blade clean on the shirt of the thug he'd stabbed, slipped it back in its sheath under his collar at the nape of his neck, and shrugged as he replied, "One must assume he no longer wished to play, hein? The last I saw of the species of insect, he was running away as if the devil incarnate was after him."

That sounded reasonable. Old Gaston didn't look scary, normally. He was much older and a lot smaller than Captain Gringo. But he looked dangerous enough, and *was,* with a knife in his hand. He fought pretty good with his feet or a gun, too.

Captain Gringo saw that both of the thugs on the ground would never bother anyone again and said, "I must be getting old. I should have known that one, there, was trying to distract me as his buddy was coming topside again."

Gaston said, "If I had not seen what was happening before *you* did, we would not be having this très amuse discussion, Dick. But if you wish to discuss it further, may one suggest we do it somewhere *else,* tout de suite?"

"Good thinking. Let's get back to the schooner before the one that got away comes back for a rematch, with company. That's where I was heading anyway, before I was so rudely interrupted."

Gaston shook his head and said, "Mais non! Not *that* way, mon hasty youth! Follow me. I have better cockroach instincts at times like these, hein?"

Captain Gringo didn't argue, at first, as he chased the little Legion deserter around a couple of corners into the dark maze of the waterfront slums of Punta Carreta. But as he started to get completely lost he grabbed Gaston's elbow and reined him to a walk, asking, "Hey, we should be clear by now. So where in the hell are we going? The docks are over *that* way, Gaston."

Gaston said, "Unhand me, you rude child. I know where the waterfront is. That is why we must go *this* way if we don't wish to be caught and hanged by our adorable necks, hein?"

"What are you talking about? Those local toughs we just tangled with didn't know we were off the *Nombre Nada.* But the one who got away has to have more friends in town than we have. So the schooner has to be the safest place for us to run for, right?"

"Wrong. The reason I was looking for you just now was to tell you not to go anywhere near that ugly little boat or your pretty gunrunning girl friend, Esperanza! It's a good thing I found you playing with those other children before you made it back, non?"

The hairs on the back of Captain Gringo's neck began to tingle. They'd been doing that a lot since the day a U.S. Army court-martial had tried to put a hangman's noose around said neck. He fell back in step with Gaston, wherever the hell they were headed, and said soberly, "Okay. Tell me exactly what happened, without all that amusing French bullshit! Have Esperanza and her crew been grabbed, and by whom?"

Gaston growled, "Merde alors, he tells one to come right to the point and then he won't shut up."

"Damm it, Gaston . . ."

"Wait. Before you strike a man old enough to be your father, your big Basque beauty and her ugly little schooner are in no danger. *They* are not wanted by anyone along this particular stretch of the Mosquito Coast. I wish one could say as much for the unruly child at my fond side, hein?"

Captain Gringo frowned and said, "I told you to cut the wisecracks. I'm not wanted here in Costa Rica either, dammit. That was the whole point in asking Esperanza to sail this way with us."

"Really? I thought the two of you had other things in mind. But perhaps it was merely the motion of the vessel that's been making her bedsprings sound like that and . . ."

Captain Gringo broke stride, spun Gaston around, and said, "Get to the fucking point."

So Gaston replied, "The U.S.S. *Maine* just dropped anchor in the harbor. Is that plain enough for you?"

Captain Gringo whistled softly. Gaston nodded and said,

"It is a bare possibility your moody Uncle Sam sent a U.S. Navy battleship into this remote banana port because their shore patrol is interested in picking bananas. But do you want to take the chance?"

"Not if I don't have to. You're sure Esperanza and the others are okay?"

Gaston tried not to look evasive as he asked, "Why would even your très fatigué former country be after Esperanza and her crew? Merde alors, half the guns she runs are for people your President Cleveland and his secret service seem fond of, for some reason that escapes me."

"I didn't ask *why* they might be after our pals, dammit. I want to know *if*! Did Esperanza *tell* you it was okay for us to just take off like this, or are you being *pratique* again?"

"We turn right at the next corner, Dick."

"You worthless little rat!"

Gaston snapped, "Fermez la bouche! You are not *that* much bigger than me, and, for a species of idiot who persists in telling me I talk too much, you certainly do listen well! I know the *Maine* is not after anyone but you, because we are on our way to meet the rogues who tipped me off in the time of Nick. One of them contacted me earlier this evening as I was scouting the paseo for a species of pussy who admires older men. They told me to warn you and meet them later at the posada I am leading you to. One assumes they have a deal to offer that has to be more enjoyable than returning to the States in irons, non?"

Captain Gringo came to another complete stop, one eyebrow raised, as he said, "I think I liked it better back there in that alley with guys I understood better. These guys contacted you over on the plaza. Have you even seen *one* guy in U.S. Navy whites in town tonight? I know I haven't!"

Gaston frowned and asked, "Are you suggesting I would be dumb enough to lead you into a trap, Dick?"

"Why not? I've been dumb enough to lead *you* into a couple. Tell me some more about these helpful pals of yours—and, by the way, have you any idea who the fuck they *are?*"

Gaston said, "Picky, picky, picky. A person is good enough to warn you of danger and you insist on a formal introduction?"

Captain Gringo didn't answer. It was just light enough to make out a drainpipe running down from a tile roof. Better yet, there were no windows on the streetside wall of the stucco house in question.

As he started hauling himself up, hand over hand, Gaston shrugged and followed. They couldn't discuss what they were doing until they'd both made it to the crunchy terra-cotta tiles of the low-pitched roof. Then Gaston asked, mildly, what they were doing up there.

Captain Gringo didn't answer as he gingerly rose to his feet for a better look across the rooftops between him and the harbor. He was more worried about cracking a tile than falling. So he told Gaston to stay put, once he spotted what he'd hoped he wouldn't see.

Then he dropped down beside the lighter Frenchman to spread his weight on the tiles before he sighed and said, "I can't swear it's the U.S.S. *Maine*. But there's a fucking big battlewagon for sure in the harbor right now. It gets worse. They're sending a steam launch ashore."

Gaston nodded and said, "Eh bien, one tends to doubt they are landing mere tourists. Would the rogues who tipped us off have done so if they were working for the U.S. Navy, Dick?"

Captain Gringo shrugged and said, "Guess not. Maybe we'd better go see who in hell they *are* working for. We can't stay here all night, and if our pals aboard the schooner have a lick of sense they'll be putting out to sea any minute!''

When they got to the posada they found out that the gang, or whatever, hadn't merely rented part of it. They'd taken over lock, stock, and barrel. A notice nailed to the front door said, in Spanish, that the inn was closed for alterations. Another sign, in English, said less politely that the joint was off limits to U.S. military personnel.

Since neither notice applied to soldiers of fortune, they went in. The main-floor cantina was dimly lit and almost deserted. A not-bad-looking ladina was reading a magazine behind the bar. A tough-looking bozo in a rumpled linen suit was seated alone at a table near the entrance, with a sawed-off shotgun and a schooner of cerveza in front of him. Four other knock-around guys were playing cards at another table across the room. They looked about as friendly as the thugs who'd jumped Captain Gringo in that alley. But Gaston recognized the two who'd contacted him earlier at the paseo. So nobody got tense when the guy with the shotgun got up to casually lock the door behind them.

One of the gunslicks who knew Gaston said, ''The big chiefs are waiting upstairs to talk to you. What took you so long?''

Gaston muttered something about the crude manners in Punta Carreta and Captain Gringo said nothing as the two of them crossed to the stairwell and went on up.

The hall above was illuminated even lousier. All the doors but one at the far end of the hall were closed. That one was open and spilling brighter light. So that's where they went.

It was obvious that two Anglo women—seated side by side

on one of the leather couches by the beehive fireplace in the parlor of the suite they'd taken—were identical twins. They were both tough-looking but not unattractive blondes who could have been either side of thirty. There was a coffee table between the facing couches, and, better yet, there was a tray of glasses and a bottle of Jamaica rum to go with them. One of the women said, "Sit down. We've been expecting you boys. You can call me Flora, and this is my sister, Dora. Not our real names, of course. We work together for obvious reasons."

Captain Gringo waited until he and Gaston were seated and Flora was pouring drinks for them before he asked who they worked for. Dora said, "It's such a bother to make up names. Let's just say my sister and I are insurance agents."

"You're out to sell us insurance, ma'am?"

Flora laughed as she handed him his drink and said, "Hardly. You boys couldn't afford the premiums our company would charge to insure anyone in your line of work. What my sister meant was that we're, ah, troubleshooters for a big American insurance firm. We want to hire you to shoot some trouble."

Captain Gringo didn't answer as he tasted his drink. It wasn't bad. Gaston smiled and said, "Forgive me, m'mselle. I find it rather odd that an insurance firm would need our usual services."

Flora said, "That's because you don't know much about life insurance, Lieutenant Verrier. Our firm made the mistake of issuing a double-indemnity policy on what they thought was a good risk. A young lady from a good Chicago meat-packing family was on her way to Europe. Our underwriters assumed she meant to take the usual grand tour, of course, when they allowed her parents to take out a rather alarming but short-term policy on her continued existence. They had no way of knowing, at the time, that the girl was gaga, see?''

Captain Gringo shook his head and said, ''I'm afraid I don't see. We're not in Europe. We're in Central America.''

''So is the nutty and overinsured meat packer's daughter,'' said Dora adding, ''She's with the International Red Cross in Guatemala, trying to get herself killed. If she manages to do it, our company is out a hundred thousand Yankee dollars. Need we say more?''

Captain Gringo said, ''I wish you would. For openers, how did you two know Gaston and I were here in Punta Carreta, and what makes you think we'd be any help to you in Guatemala?''

Flora said, ''We were waiting for you in Limón, knowing you were on your way back to Costa Rica after that last job. We found out the U.S. Navy was keeping tabs on your career, too. So we rode down the coast like hell, and fortunately got here faster than the *Maine*. Never mind how we read the U.S. Navy's mail. As to your qualifications, do you recall the lady named Vera, who works for Lloyd's of London?''

''Very fondly. Is she the one who recommended us?''

Dora giggled and said, ''In more ways than one. We insurance agents work together now and again, and Vera told us how understanding you were that time in Nicaragua.''

Flora said, ''You saved Lloyd's a bundle by taking out those crooks in such a delicate manner. This job we have for you may involve the same kind of work. Would you like to see the machine gun we bought for you now?''

Since she was rising, Captain Gringo rose too. On her feet, Flora was something worth rising for. She had to be wearing a corset under that thin summer print. No mortal woman could have a natural waistline that slender if her other parts were real. She probably had some bracing for those big knockers, too. They were riding high, considering their size.

She led him into another, darker room and struck a match to light a candle on a large round table in the center of the room. The candle was not alone. A Maxim .30-30 was perched on its tripod mount atop the table. It was covered with shipping grease and looked spanking new. He nodded approvingly, stepped over to it, and opened the breech to inspect it as he asked where the ammo belts were. She said, "Under the table. As you see, we haven't cleaned it or messed with the head spacing. Our game is insurance. We leave weaponry to former weapons officers."

"Oh, you know about my past?"

"Did you think we hired people we didn't know about? Please don't tell me you were framed by the U.S. Army, Dick. Every gunslick we meet seems to have been framed for some damned thing or another, and it gets to be a bore. We know you've been a good boy since you escaped from that army guardhouse in the States. Can I cable the home office you've taken the job?"

He said, "Maybe. Let's talk some more about the fine print. Where's Gaston, by the way?"

"With Dora. I won the toss. We can talk more comfortably in the next room, and I see you're going to take some convincing."

He followed her as she picked up the candle and led the way into yet another room. When he saw the four-poster and nothing else to sit on, he smiled thinly and asked, "Is your sister trying to convince Gaston, Flora?"

She laughed and said, "I told you she lost the toss. Why don't we get the sexual tension out of the way before I explain just what else I want you to do for us, dear?"

Before he could answer, Flora slipped her dress over her

head and sat on the bed to unpin her hair. He repressed a gasp of delighted surprise when he saw she wasn't wearing another stitch, save for her long black stockings and high-button shoes. He'd been wrong about her needing whalebone underwear. Flora was built like an impossibly constructed brick shithouse. So what in the hell was he doing with his own duds on at a time like this?

It took him only a little longer to shuck everything but his socks and hang his shoulder rig within easy reach of the bed as the statuesque brunette lay back across it. But, though he was already rising to the occasion, Captain Gringo didn't like surprises. So he moved over to lock the door from the inside before he turned to join her. As he did so, she smiled up at him and said, "Vera told us you had amazing self-control." Then, as she glanced down between them, she gasped and added, "Oh, my God, she might have warned me about *that*!"

He said, "Flattery will get you everywhere," as he reclined beside her, took her in his arms, and kissed her while he ran his free hand down her roller-coaster curves to warm her up a bit, first.

When his hand got to home plate, he saw she didn't need much foreplay. Her love maw was almost gushing. So, as she tongued him deeply, he just rolled into the saddle between her welcoming thighs and commenced to enter her.

It wasn't as easy as he'd expected. Despite her Junoesque hips and expectant lubrication, old Flora was built sort of tight. She seemed more than willing to help him get it in, judging from the way she opened wide and said "Ah!"; but it felt like a ten-year-old virgin had somehow managed to get inside the body of a more than full-grown woman and he was afraid that if he really shoved hard he could hurt her.

She seemed worried about it too, and moaned, "Jesus,

take it easy, handsome. I haven't been with a man for months and . . . Forget what I just said. Vera was right. It only seems impossible at first.''

He chuckled fondly as he finally got it all the way in, let her get used to it, and started moving gently. She wrapped her silk-sheathed legs around him with a contented sigh and purred, ''Oh, yesss! I like tall men, don't you?''

''Not this way. It works better when one of us is a girl. So what's with the other dame in Guatemala, Flora?''

''Fuck her. Better yet, fuck me! I'll tell you about the job later, after you do a job on me, you goof!''

That sounded reasonable. So he started moving faster. She did, too, and though she stayed just as tight after she came ahead of him, her insides were even wetter now, so he could pound her harder without rubbing either of them raw. It seemed to be driving her nuts.

She sobbed, ''Oh, God, I'm so glad I won the toss! Poor Dora doesn't know what she's missing!''

He didn't say he doubted that. He knew there was more to Gaston than met the eye, and, from the way women pestered Gaston, once he'd shown them that dirty old men needed love and respect, too, Captain Gringo suspected old Dora was in for what old Queen Victoria regarded as crimes against nature. Captain Gringo was as depraved as the average good sport, but Gaston would eat anything, like a maniac.

The twin sister Captain Gringo was enjoying seemed to be a maniac too, now that she'd gotten over her first shyness with him. She was moving under him amazingly as he came, hard, and let it soak in her a moment as he got his second wind. She moved so well it hardly mattered that he wasn't. She gasped and said, ''I can't believe your stamina, darling. Most men are such quitters!''

He repressed a grimace and didn't answer. He could see

how a dame like Flora could have a problem keeping the
average guy going. Between her not bad looks, the way she
moved them, and the usual tightness between her shapely
hugging thighs, Flora could have made a fortune in Dodge
any night the herds were in town. She was a born three-
minute trick.

He was saved from looking like a sissy to her because of
reasons he didn't think it proper to discuss with a lady. He'd
been cruising up the Mosquito Coast, until this evening, with
a hell of a good lay named Esperanza. So he'd started with
the advantage of not being as hard up as the average guy old
Flora had probably crossed sex organs with in her travels.

He could tell she'd done so with many a man in her
checkered past. Few professional whores moved half as well.
But he made no value judgments about his hyperactive
partner of the moment. For in his own time he'd screwed
around more than the queen approved of, and, what the hell,
she wasn't charging for such nice stuff. Or was she?

Knowing what had to be coming, besides Flora, distracted
him enough to keep him moving in her at a steady lope
without coming again, as he pondered on what else he and
Gaston might be getting into. She seemed to take his cool,
protracted lovemaking as a compliment, since she came
again, or said she had. He decided he might as well join her
and started pounding harder. She pleaded, "Please, Dick! I'm
too sensitized to do it again. Don't you want to hear about the
job in Guatemala now?"

He didn't answer. He was almost there, and, Jesus, it was
even better this time. She moaned that he was hurting her as
she thrust her pelvis up to take it all. As he shot deep within
her, she sobbed and said, "Oh, Christ, me too! You're killing
me and I love every inch of it!"

He laughed, rolled off, and said, "Okay, let's talk. I have a smoke in my shirt pocket, if I can remember where the hell I dropped my damned shirt.''

As he sat up and bent over to pick up his shirt from the floor by the bed, Flora sighed and said, ''God, you have a lovely body. But as I was saying, this stupid lady from Chicago is insured double indemnity against a violent death.''

''What happens if she just catches consumption?''

''It only costs us half as much, of course. She's young, healthy, and our company doctors checked her lungs before we insured her. We naturally assumed we were talking about a little Miss Rich Bitch who intended to take in a few cathedrals and art museums before she came back to Chicago to settle down as a spoiled society matron. So we gave her goddamned parents good terms on her goddamned policy. It was low premium and short term. Fifty thou' should she croak of natural causes while out of the States. Double that, should she be eaten by cannibals, murdered for her shoes in Paris, or something. I mean, how many rich American tourists die of anything while they take the usual grand lux tour, right?''

He got a claro and some waterproof matches from his shirt, lit up, and leaned back to rejoin Flora as he asked, ''Two questions. Are all bets off once she returns to the States, and what in the hell is she doing in Guatemala if she said she was going to Europe?''

Flora snuggled closer and said, ''I told you the policy was short term. No definite dates, since our underwriters assumed she'd just nip over for the summer and be back in time for the social season. Our legal eagles have studied the question of her destination. We're stuck. She did go to Europe. She hasn't been back to the States in over two years. The stupid little do-gooder joined the International Red Cross when she got to Geneva. Her meat-packing papa says he had no idea his daughter was out to save the world, the lying son of a bitch. He took out a bargain double indemnity on her because he knew she might not be long for this world. When we checked further, as we should have in the first place, we found out she's always been a tomboy who worried her folks sick. While she was still a damned teen-ager she tore off to Apache country to do social work among the Pueblo Indians!''

He whistled softly and said, ''You wouldn't have her as a client right now if she'd gone out to serve tea to the *noisier* New Mexican tribes. But how much trouble can even a tomboy get into as a Red Cross nurse?''

''You want it alphabetical or numerical? You know, of course, that the Guatemalan highlands are infested with bandits and active volcanoes?''

''So's the rest of Central America. Though most of the volcanoes I've met have been quiet, so far.''

''That's what Vera told me, bless her. But while the volcano you and Gaston met that time in Nicaragua for Lloyd's was a sleeping giant, there's one in Guatemala that's a pisser. They call if Boca-Bruja. It's up near the Mexican border and it's just blown its top. Earthquakes, ashfall, lava flows, the works. The International Red Cross sent a medical-rescue team into the disaster area a few weeks ago, and guess who went with them?''

''Ouch. What's her name?''

''Cynthia Swann, of the Chicago Swanns, the silly little bitch. We have to get her out of there before she manages to get herself killed by Boca-Bruja or that even sillier Caballero Blanco.''

''What in the hell is Caballero Blanco? I mean, I know it means 'White Knight,' but—''

''Don't ask *me* why he thinks he's a white knight,'' she cut in, adding, ''He's the local rebel leader, bandit leader, or both. Whatever he is, he's got the Guatemalan government worried. He and that damned volcano have my company worried, too. We want you to go in and get our overinsured client out, Dick. What's it going to cost us?''

"Let's worry about that after I decide on the job. What if this client of yours doesn't want to come out with us? We're soldiers of fortune, not white slavers.''

Flora began to toy with his limp tool as he smoked the firmer claro while she explained, "They'll all want to come out, if anyone can get into them. The last anyone heard from the team, they were low on supplies, the natives were restless, and they'd done all they could.''

"I know the feeling. So what's stopping the Red Cross team from just packing it in and returning to civilization on their own?''

"They can't. They're cut off. The only mountain trail in or out of the disaster area isn't there anymore. It seems to be covered with lava, a lake of boiling acid water, or both. Reports are naturally a little sketchy at the moment.''

By this time she'd taken the matter firmly in hand and it was starting to get firm indeed as she stroked it skillfully. He said, "Hold it. Better yet, let go. It's hard to talk sense with a hard-on, and I'm missing something here. You say you want us to go in and get them out. Then you say the only trail in or out is covered by lava and boiling acid. I'm good, honey, but I'm not *that* good!''

"You're marvelous,'' she purred. As she went on playing with him, she explained, "I said the trail from the Guatemalan lowlands was cut off. I didn't say it was the only one. Some Mexican smugglers tell us there's another trail into the disaster area, through the Mexican border country.''

He frowned and said, "Ouch! Not what you're doing to my dong. I meant the country you're talking about. Mexico makes me nervous, doll. Sometimes I think I make El Presidente Diaz nervous too. Every time I go anywhere near Mexico, his damned rurales wind up trying to shoot my ears off!''

''That's why we got you the Maxim in the next room, dear. We tried to reason with El Presidente, too. But the prick won't cooperate, and, hmm, speaking of cooperative pricks...''

''Not just yet, dammit! You know I'm willing to screw you all night, Flora. But I'm starting to wonder about less attractive kinds of screwing. I'm missing something. The Diaz dictatorship can be rude as hell to widows and orphans, but that oily old bastard running it likes to stay in good with Uncle Sam if it doesn't cost him anything, and I don't see why he'd refuse to allow an American insurance company to do things the easier way. So what's all this bullshit with machine guns and soldiers of fortune los rurales have orders to shoot on sight?''

''Oh, for God's sake, Dick, if this was a ruse to capture you and Gaston, we'd have just let the shore patrol from the *Maine* pick you up.''

''We knew that or we wouldn't have come to meet you. Uncle Sam's reward on my head is bigger than the one Diaz has offered, too. But I still don't see why you can't just send in a plain old rescue team.''

''Diaz won't let us. He says he can't be responsible for the lives of his Yanqui guests in country he doesn't control, see?''

''No, I don't see. The last time I visited Mexico, old Diaz was in a lot more control than most Mexicans with any brains wanted him to be. He's got his butchering rurales *everywhere*, Flora!''

She said, ''Not in the south Sierra Madres near the Guatemalan border, dear. What there is of the country on the map is mighty rugged, and a lot of it's not on any map. Our agents in Mexico City say El Presidente could be telling the truth for a change. No rurales have been patrolling that far south in some time. The last bunch they sent in never came out. So you and Gaston won't have to worry about rurales, see?''

"Jesus, what *do* we have to worry about, if it eats *rurales* for breakfast? Those apes are *tough*!''

"Pretty please with sugar and a new machine gun on it? We'll have Mexican guides waiting for you, and we can promise a safe landing on a stretch of the southwest Mexican coast that another agent of ours controls better than El Presidente Diaz might suspect.''

"I'll think about it,'' he growled, as she dropped her head in his lap to arouse him even more with her soft, moist, tightly pursed lips. He knew she couldn't talk with her mouth so full and he didn't feel like discussing business at a time like this. So he chuckled and said, "Hey, let's not waste it. I want some more of the real thing, doll box!''

She giggled and rose to her hands and knees to swivel around. She might have meant to lie down again, but he had a better idea when he saw how nice her curvaceous derriere looked by candlelight. So he swung off the bed, grabbed a hip bone with each hand as he turned to aim his weapon, and, standing in his stocking feet on the floor, pulled her on like a glove, dog-style.

She arched her spine to take it all the way as she gasped, "Oh, yessss! It feels even deeper that way. I wonder if you'd even need a machine gun to get through the Sierra Madres, darling. I'll bet if you just pointed that big cock at half the bandits in Mexico they'd run away screaming!''

He laughed, but said, "I'm more worried about the ones

who *don't* run away. If we have to discuss business at such a weird time, what are you offering, besides *this*, Flora?''

"What you're doing to me is hardly a matter I'd want on the company books, you big goof. I was told to offer you the going soldier-of-fortune monthly fee or a flat rate, whichever you prefer. Ah, could you move a little faster?"

He did, as he thought for a few strokes and then said, "Okay. We charge a thousand a month, each. If it takes us a whole month to get in and out, we're probably not going to get in or out. How does a flat two thou', one now and one if we make it, sound to you, Flora?''

"Oooh! Just keep going in and out like that and you've got a deal! That feels fantastic!"

Everything about her and the company she worked for seemed a little fantastic. But, up to now, it sure felt good. He asked her, "Will you and your sister be going with us, Flora?''

She said, "No, damm it. Our job is finished once we get you boys over to the Pacific coast and turn you over to other company people. But if I can't *go* with you, I sure am *coming* with you and, Jesusssss!"

She fell off him, forward, leaving him in mid-air, halfway to heaven. He started to drop back into position atop her, but Flora rolled to one side and said, "That's enough for now, dear. I have to get dressed and start the ball rolling.''

"Can't you roll your balls after I ball you at least one more time, dammit? I was about to come, honey!''

She laughed, jumped up, and then bent to pick up the cigar he'd dropped on the bare floor as she said, "I'll be right back, silly. Here, smoke this or something until I send a few messages. Please don't jerk off while I'm gone, though. I'm still hot, too.''

He laughed, accepted the smoke like a good sport, and relit

it as she quickly slipped her print dress back on and sort of pinned her hair. He said, "I still have to check with Gaston. But if your sister's as persuasive as you are, I don't think he'll give us any argument. We don't have anyplace better to go, now that we can't get back to the waterfront. How do we get over to the other coast?"

She said she'd tell him later and left him alone. He took a deep puff of smoke as he lay back across the bed, and damned if he didn't still have a full erection. He laughed again. He knew why she'd cut him off like that. She didn't intend to start from scratch when she came back. Yeah, she'd been around a few blocks with the other boys on the block. But was that anything to bitch about?

He wondered how long it was going to take her. The old posada didn't have electricity, let alone a telephone. But there was a cable office in town and she'd surely send one of her armed brownies instead of going out alone after dark, unescorted, in a little Hispanic town.

He wondered why he was wondering. He'd had the hot-blooded Basque beauty, Esperanza, shortly after sunrise that morning. It wasn't that long after sunset, and he'd just had strange stuff. Either of them were enough to satisfy a sensible man for at least a couple of days, and this particular day had been sort of rough.

He snuffed out the cigar again. It was dangerous to smoke in bed when a guy felt like he'd been digging ditches. Some bruises he'd picked up in that alley fight were coming back to haunt him now, and he sure hoped old Flora wouldn't feel insulted if she found him asleep when she got back. He wasn't sure it was safe to doze off here and now. But where the hell else in town would it be safer?

He was just about to when the door opened and a familiar teasing voice said, "Oh, dear, you've let it go soft, you brute. Have you been naughty while I was confirming your contract, or are you simply tired of me already?''

He opened one eye and growled, ''Come over here and find out how weak and helpless I am, doll box. Did the front office say when I get to see any of your other charms?''

She stripped even faster than the last time, and as she got on the bed with him he noticed she'd taken time to get rid of her stockings and those damned high heels, bless her. She cuddled beside him and reached for his groin as she said, ''We'll give you boys your checks in the morning before you catch the coach to San José. I don't have my fountain pen or anything *else* on me at the moment.''

He laughed, said that was for damned sure, and reeled her in for a kiss. He wasn't sure if he meant it or not. She'd left him way in the middle of the air, but now that he'd had time to cool down, his back sure felt stiff.

She kissed back, passionately enough to inform him that if *he'd* had enough, *she* surely hadn't. She tongued him and did other things as teasing with her soft, experienced hand. So maybe his back wasn't that stiff after all. He was getting stiff enough where it mattered.

But she must have been a perfectionist. She withdrew her tongue, sat up, and said, ''The poor thing seems to be injured. Mommy had better kiss it and make it well.''

That seemed fair. It seemed even better when she went down on him again and commenced to play French music even better than his old meat flute remembered. He wondered if she expected him to return the favor. Esperanza usually did, but Esperanza hadn't been laying anyone else of late, and though Flora *said* she hadn't been with another man for some time, he found it hard to buy. No lady screwed that good without constant practice, and, hell, he hadn't even had to ask. He could imagine who or what she might go to bed with if he, or *it,* really begged for it!

But she didn't offer him any seafood. She simply sucked it to full attention and then forked a shapely and now naked thigh across him to straddle him as she said, "I like it best on top. Just lie still, dear. This freak of nature you carry in your pants takes a little getting used to."

He didn't answer. He just lay supine, not moving anything, as she began slowly and teasingly to impale herself on his now raging erection. As she did so, her eyes got wider and she hissed, "Oh, I don't know, dear. This is really a little too much of a good thing, if you ask me!"

He hadn't asked her. He'd thought they'd gotten beyond that maidenly crap by now. But damned if she didn't feel even tighter as she gingerly settled down, biting her lower lip as if she were getting into a hot bath she wasn't sure she could stand.

Apparently she could. Because once it was all the way in she leaned forward and started moving her hips very nicely indeed. Now he was glad he hadn't fallen asleep. They hadn't tried it this way before, and it felt completely different. He reached up to fondle her breasts as she started bouncing faster. That was funny. He hadn't noticed, the last time, that one of Flora's nipples was inverted. But the little mole he had noticed at the base of Flora's throat seemed to be missing, and so, what in the hell were they up to if this was *Dora?*

He knew that was a dumb question as soon as he asked it of himself. *He* was blessed with natural curiosity. Why should dames be all that different? Obviously the dizzy twins had compared notes on more than their report to the home office, and the guy who'd said variety was the spice of life had had a good point. It was sort of flattering to know old Flora had recommended him so highly as she took her turn learning about French culture. He wondered if Gaston would catch on as quickly. He hoped not. He decided not to tell him if he didn't. Even Gaston had some standards, and Captain Gringo knew he'd be mad as hell if he found out he'd just eaten out a broad who'd come more than once with another guy.

Dora, still pretending to be Flora, moaned that she was too excited to go on that way. So he rolled her over to do it right, and, yeah, now he knew for sure.

The two girls had the same faces and bodies. They were even built much the same between their identical thighs. But this one moved nothing like her twin sister. She was not only more acrobatic, she was double-jointed as well, he learned, as she locked one ankle around the nape of his neck and proceeded to run her bare toes through his hair while she fondled his nuts with one hand and tried to sodomize him with one finger of the other.

He told her he didn't enjoy that. She giggled and said lots of men did and that she wanted to find out if his rectum was as tight as her pussy. He laughed and told her nothing was as tight as her pussy. If she got the joke, she went on playing dumb, until they'd both enjoyed themselves beyond passion into just plain showing off.

He knew she was waiting for him to call a halt. So he did, got up to make sure the door was locked, and staggered back to bed. They were both asleep within minutes.

Captain Gringo would have slept until noon, if the lady in bed with him had let him. But as the tropic sun peeped through the jalousie slats across the window, she nudged him awake and said they had to think about getting up and dressed if he expected to eat any breakfast before the stage to the high country pulled out.

He groaned, sat up, and looked around for something to put on. She lay there, stark naked, looking a little hurt as she asked, "Just like that? We'll probably never meet again, and you don't even want to screw me good-bye properly?"

She did look tempting with the strips of sunlight painting tiger stripes across her naked flesh like that, and now that he reconsidered his options, he did have a morning hard-on. So he laughed, kissed her, and laughed even harder when he mounted her. She naturally asked why, and he naturally didn't tell her he'd just noticed that her mole was back and both her nipples were normal again this morning. Considering what Gaston had probably been doing to her tight little twat in recent memory, it was mighty flattering to know she'd come back for another old-fashioned lay with him.

Of course, Dora was probably enjoying this weird game of musical beds right now, too, if he knew Gaston. So he just humped away and went along with the harmless gag. He enjoyed amusing sex adventures as well as the next guy or gal.

But all good things must come to an end, and once they'd kissed the girls good-bye and boarded the San José stage with their gear, the rest of the day was boring as hell.

Costa Rica had nice scenery, a stable popular government, and not enough bandits along its dirt-paved coach roads to matter. The coaches were no better or worse than any others. There was no such thing as a comfortable stagecoach and it took forever to get up to the cooler high country.

They spent the night at a highland posada, with no other company, then spent another boring day getting to San José. Then things got better for a while. They cashed the checks the twins had given them, banked most of it, got laid, and caught the train down to the Pacific seaport of Puntarenas. They didn't meet anyone pretty enough to matter on the train, nobody shot at them along the way, and while the train wasn't a Pullman, it sure beat a coach in every way.

In Puntarenas they were met at the depot by a couple of gun thugs who said they were working for the same insurance company and probably were, because they helped Captain Gringo and Gaston with their considerable luggage and drove them to the docks where a steel-hulled schooner was waiting. Captain Gringo asked the bored-looking Yankee skipper if they had to worry about clearing customs and the skipper shifted the toothpick in his mouth to the other side and told him not to be silly. So the next thing the two soldiers of fortune knew, they'd been shown to not-great but not-bad staterooms and were on their way.

The voyage up the Pacific coast was a lot more comfortable than either a coach or train, but it seemed to be taking forever, so things tended to even out. The food, like everything else aboard the chartered schooner, was neither good nor bad. The crewmen, while polite enough, were either uncommunicative by nature or, more probably, under orders not to discuss company business with temporary help.

Gaston made up for it by talking a blue streak, as usual. So far, his only comment on the twins back in Costa Rica had been to the effect that the one he'd had had been almost too much for a man his age. His younger American friend preferred to leave him in ignorant bliss and kept changing the subject to where they were going rather than where they'd just been. Hence, long before they got there, Captain Gringo heard more about the Mexican-Guatemalan border country than he really felt the need to know.

Gaston, of course, knew Mexico like the back of his hand, having knocked around it since back in the seventies, fighting for various sides in the unsettled years since Juarez had died and left the place in one hell of a mess.

Gaston hadn't passed through the particular part of Mexico they were headed for in *recent* memory. But he remembered it, not too fondly, from the time he'd been part of a French Foreign Legion border patrol for the late Emperor Maximilian of Mexico, and, as Gaston asked rhetorically, how much could the amusingly eroded scablands of the southern Sierra Madres have improved in a generation?

He added that the Sierra Madres paid no attention to any border drawn by human hands on any map. They simply ran on down through Central America, with a modest gap here and there, until they turned into the Andes of South America. Some parts were higher and some parts were lower, but the mountain chain was all rough-and-ready rock laced with live volcanoes, carved with deep canyons, and shaken with monotonous regularity by earthquakes. He said he had no idea why any sensible person would want to live in such country.

Captain Gringo said, "Never mind the geology lecture and let's not worry about sensible people. What do you know about more truculent mountaineers, Gaston?"

The Frenchman shrugged and replied, "The last time we marched through, they shot at us avec annoying accuracy. We did not get to talk to many of the natives. For some reason they did not regard us as the liberators Maximilian insisted we were. One must assume, since El Presidente Diaz is an even bigger species of bastard, they have not changed much more than their adorable mountains."

Captain Gringo nodded and said, "The twins said the country was too rough for los rurales to police. What do you make of this white knight character, Gaston?"

Gaston shrugged and said, "He sounds like the usual Mexican guerrilla with perhaps unusual taste in attire."

"Hold it. El Caballero Blanco's not supposed to be raising hell on the *Mexican* side of the border, remember?"

"I remember, but does El Caballero Blanco? The so-called border is an imaginary line on a map this species of pale idiot may not have ever read, if indeed he can read at all. You will see when we get there, assuming we ever get there, that there shall be neither a border fence nor a sign welcoming us to Guatemala. It's the kind of country your old friend Geronimo would love to meet you in for a rematch. As a matter of fact, now that I think back, Geronimo could have some distant cousins already there, waiting for us. I forget the names of the local tribes. But I seem to recall they were poor relations of the Aztec, Maya, or some other dreadful Indians."

"So what? By now they've been converted by missionaries, right?"

"Surely you jest. I just told you those hills were not safe for either the French Foreign Legion or los rurales! To convert a savage to anything, one must first get close enough to talk to him, alive."

Captain Gringo knew better than to ask about the so-called Spanish conquest. But Gaston tended to pontificate about watch repair when all you'd asked him was the time of day. So the little Frenchman insisted on explaining, "The conquistadores tended to skip the tribes who had no gold. So a lot of places that appear on the map as former Spanish colonies are still inhabited by people who never heard of His Most Catholic Majesty and . . ."

"Never mind the history lesson," Captain Gringo cut in, adding, "I get the picture. Wild Indians don't scare me as much as wilder bandits with modern weapons. What's the bandit situation in the Sierra Madres right now?"

"Right now? Merde alors, it's been over twenty years, Dick. Since the country is très rustique, one may assume anyone dwelling in the scablands wearing pants and guns would tend to be antisocial, hein?"

"The twins said the guys who'll be meeting us up the coast are Mexican smugglers who know the way into the Guatemalan version of the Sierra Madres. Does that make sense to you?"

Gaston shrugged and observed, "To indulge in smuggling, one would have to know the way across *some* border or other, non?"

"Maybe. But what in the hell would they be smuggling? Guatemala is a poor country. Even if it wasn't, the Guatemalans grow the same crops, drink the same coffee, and smoke the same weeds."

Gaston laughed and said, "Eh bien, that is easy to answer, Dick. Our smugglers will most obviously be running silver into Guatemala and guns into Mexico on the return trip. El Presidente Diaz has an annoying habit of demanding one-fifth of all minerals exported from Mexico, and of course he takes a très dim view of anyone importing guns into his private paradise for peons."

Captain Gringo thought, nodded, and said, "Yeah, that works. If the guides the company's hired jump the border regularly, they must have some sort of arrangement with the local Indian and mestizo types. So the only question left before the house is how far we can trust our guides, right?"

Gaston grimaced and said, "That is no question. Never trust any stranger with a gun. Have you considered the très obvious easy way out yet, my donquichottesque child?"

Captain Gringo shook his head and said, "It won't work any better. We can't get off this boat until it docks, and once we're ashore in Mexico, we'll already have all the enemies we need without having to double-cross anyone. The insurance company has the local law fixed. But they won't stay fixed very long unless we carry out our part of the bargain."

"True, up to a point. My plan was to go along with the joke until we'd cleared the seaport they control. Once in the foothills of the Sierra Madres, if we cut north instead of south . . .''

"Are you crazy? That would mean playing tag with los rurales again!"

"Oui, but in much nicer country. We only have to make it as far as Tehuantepec, where the women are beautiful, the pulque is drinkable, and I know rogues who can get us aboard a southbound boat."

"You asshole. Have you forgotten there's a federale army post in Tehuantepec?"

"Sacre goddamn, Dick. I said nothing about reporting in to the duty sergeant there. The shitty species of town is trés lousy with all sorts of unwashed beachcombers of various complexions. Who is going to notice two more, if we don't stay long?"

"The guides the insurance company's hired, of course. They've just paid us the front money, in case you forgot, and somehow I have a pretty good suspicion they'll want to protect their investment."

Gaston shrugged and said, "The guides are no problem. As for the front money, we have already cashed our checks. So what could they do about it, once we were safely back in San José?"

"Back up and run that shit about our guides past me again. Are you suggesting what it sounds like you're suggesting, you murderous little bastard?"

"Oui, but would it not make more sense to murder *them* before they can murder us? What hold can the insurance company have on them, once they have us at their mercy in the high country? If they make a regular habit of passing through it, they must have lots of friends there, non?"

"Okay, but . . ."

"But me no buts, Dick. We are discussing professional

criminals on their own home grounds. The insurance company could hardly have offered them more than they just paid us. The machine gun, ammo, and other supplies we're packing in could be sold for much more to any of a dozen Mexican rebel factions. Merde alors, we'd be trusting them with our lives in a savage area where most men would kill a stranger for his shoes, or just for practice!''

Captain Gringo fished out a claro, lit it, and blew a thoughtful smoke ring before he said, ''You've got more than a point. But let's not cross our bridges before we're even ashore. We'll play it by ear as we go. If the guides act reasonable, we'll go along with the gag. If they stare too much at our mosquito boots, we'll do it your way.''

''Dick, a ladrón out to rob you seldom tells you in advance.''

''I've noticed that. I'm still not about to gun anyone who hasn't given me a good reason.''

''Eh bien, what are we arguing about, then? I shall watch the sons of the bitch while you are sleeping. You shall watch the sons of the bitch while I am sleeping. When they prove me right, we shall kill the sons of the bitch and cut this shit of the bull, hein?''

The Yankee skipper had timed it so that the schooner put into the fishing village and former pirate cove after dark. The shoreline was ringed with lantern light since, like most people in the tropics, the local Mexicans were night people. But the skipper wasn't interested in the dimmer illumination. He waited until someone ashore flashed a bull's-eye lantern at him exactly twice, then thrice, before he dropped anchor, well out in the harbor roads.

Captain Gringo and Gaston went aft to the poop to ask him what happened next. The laconic New Englander spat over the side and said, "We wait until they send out a lighter for you and your gear. We don't wait long. They sent the right signal. But I don't like the looks of them other two vessels, yonder."

They followed his gaze shoreward and could just make out the black outlines of two moored vessels, both bigger than the one they were on. Captain Gringo squinted and said, "I make the one closer in a three-island tramp steamer. The other sure looks a lot like a gunboat. Would it be Mexican, skipper?"

"How the hell should I know? Never seen it in these waters before. Never seen this port so crowded before, neither. Don't like it. But a deal's a deal and they did signal us right. So I'll give 'em a few minutes. Not too damned *many,* though. Ain't been paid enough to tangle with no gunboat, Mexican or, hell, *Bulgarian!*"

Gaston said, "Regardez, a steam launch approaches," and the skipper said, "I see it. Ain't the lighter I was expecting, neither dammit to hell. What have you boys gotten us into?"

Captain Gringo said, "I'm not sure. Could I borrow that hat of yours, skipper?"

"My hat? What in the hell do you want with my hat, Mr. Walker?"

"That's a U.S. Navy captain's gig, or I'll eat it, and your hat, bill and all. It's too late to run for it and my blond hair shows in the moonlight. You don't look like anyone they could be after."

The older man handed his merchant officer's cap to Captain Gringo, saying, "I sure hope you're a good talker. It's you they'll question when they see you on this poop with this skipper's cap."

Captain Gringo said, "I used to be an officer," as he put

the rather greasy cap on and pulled the bill low. Gaston said
something about inspecting the cargo and headed forward to
make himself scarce. A few minutes later, the padded bow of
the steam launch bumped the steel hull of the schooner, near
the sea ladder, and a voice called out, "Ensign Westfield,
U.S. Navy. Permission to come aboard?"

The real skipper muttered, "Oh, Jesus!" as Captain Gringo called back, "Permission granted, swabby. Sorry we can't
pipe you aboard fancy, but this is a working vessel, not a
seagoing show-off."

The older American at his side whispered. "Have you gone
crazy, Walker?"

Captain Gringo laughed and said, "No talking on my
bridge, mister. Just go along with me for now and I'll show
you how to deal with junior officers."

"You're going to make him *mad*, dammit!"

"Hold the thought. He's coming aboard, with company."

The white-clad ensign had two enlisted men, with pistol
belts and SP armbands on, to keep him company as he came
up the ladder and strode pompously aft. Captain Gringo
moved forward to stare coldly down at them from the poop as
he said, "Well, I see you made her up the ladder without
your mama's help, sonny. What can we do for you?"

"My captain's compliments, and we'd like to ask a few
questions, ah, sir."

"You got a search warrant, sonny?"

The young ensign snapped, "Look, I'm trying to be polite,
but I don't like to be called sonny and there's a full-grown
gun turret trained on your vessel, if you get my meaning."

Captain Gringo snorted in disgust and said, "Bullshit. This
is a Yankee schooner with proper registration and a license to
trade in these waters. You may scare Uncle Sam's little brown
brothers. But you don't look like much to *us!* Before you

hand me any more bullshit, it's only fair to warn you I served a hitch in the service one time. So I know the standing orders better than you do, sonny.''

The pissed-off ensign sniffed and said, ''I take it you were an enlisted man, of course?''

Captain Gringo laughed and said, ''Damned A. Chief petty officer, before I wised up and got out of your chickenshit school for seagoing servants. I haven't had to *sir* one of you jerk-offs for some time. But I'll be a good sport and meet you halfway if you'll tell me what the fuck you want.''

The two enlisted men behind the pompous young officer were trying not to laugh as he threw back his shoulders and said, ''That's better. My orders are to ascertain what this vessel is doing in these waters.''

Captain Gringo turned to the real skipper at his side and asked, ''Don't they teach them to talk pretty at Annapolis?'' Then he turned back to the navy men and said, ''What we're up to is none of your fucking business. But I'll tell you anyway, because you're so pretty in them tropic whites. We put in here to pick up a passenger. She'll be out here soon or we'll be leaving without her.''

''She?'' asked the ensign with a puzzled frown. Captain Gringo *wanted* the navy to stay puzzled and, hopefully, distracted, so he answered, ''Yep. Can't tell you what she looks like or how she feels about sailors. They just told us she wants to go up the coast to Mazatlán. You can't get there by land, as you'd know if you ever read your charts.''

''I know Mazatlán is cut off from the inland by mountains, dammit. Never mind your Mexican passengers. Are you *landing* anyone or anything here?''

''Who wants to know? Are you a Mexican customs officer? I'd have taken you for U.S. Navy. I sure hope you haven't boarded me under false pretenses, sonny. What the hell are *you* guys doing in this port, by the way?"

"I'll ask the questions here, if you don't mind."

"I do mind, sonny. This ain't your yard I'm anchored in. You're just down here showing the stars and stripes to the natives, and I ain't no native. So don't try to push an old sea lawyer around. You're talking to a licensed master of the U.S. Merchant Marine. So if you don't want to talk polite, get the fuck off my vessel!"

By now the two tougher shore patrolmen were grinning at each other behind their officer's back. The ensign was smart enough to know he was being made a fool of, too. But, as Captain Gringo had hoped, he didn't know what he could do about it.

He said, "Very well. I'll inform my commanding officer how you feel about the U.S. Navy and we shall see what we shall see."

Captain Gringo chuckled indulgently and said, "Oh, hell, I don't want a war with you, sonny. Just so we understand I don't *have* to take no shit off you, I'll let you see our papers and show you the cargo manifest. My mate here has 'em."

He turned to the real skipper and said, "Show junior our papers, Smitty?"

The Yankee skipper swore under his breath and said, "They're in my desk, ah, Skipper."

Captain Gringo shrugged and said, "Go get 'em, then. May as well send these boys away happy."

The real skipper moved for the nearest hatchway, fast, as Captain Gringo told the navy boarding party they could smoke if they had 'em, and asked casually, "Have you checked out that cargo vessel closer to shore yet? Now *there's* a tub that could be landing all sorts of awful things, if you ask me."

The ensign laughed and said, "A lot you know. We just escorted it down from San Diego. It's a Red Cross mercy ship. You've heard about the earthquakes and ashfalls not far from here?"

"Heard something about something like that in the hills of Guatemala. But this is *Mexico,* mister."

Relieved not to be called sonny, the ensign nodded and explained, "You can't get into the disaster area from Guatemala. The newer and bigger team means to try getting in from the north."

"No shit? Well, I'm glad I'm not going with 'em. Hear it's mighty rough country, inland from here. I hope, for their sake, it's a big expedition with lots of guns."

"It's not the navy's problem, once they're all safely ashore and on their way."

"How come you had to escort 'em down the coast, then? I've never met with coastal pirates in these waters, mister."

The ensign grimaced and said, "The biggest pirate in Mexico seems to be running the country at the moment. President Cleveland himself asked Diaz to allow the International Red Cross to enter the disaster area via Mexican territory, and the greaser said *no!*"

Captain Gringo laughed and said, "I figured there had to be some reason for a gunboat in this harbor. Ain't it a bitch how reasonable some old boys can get when you're pointing four-inchers at 'em?"

The ensign said it was nice to see they agreed on *some* things, and so, by the time the real skipper came warily back with the ship's papers, they were on somewhat friendlier terms. The ensign scanned the papers in the poor light, as if he knew what he was reading. Captain Gringo knew he'd go back to his gunboat to report that he'd checked them out, if only to look more important than they'd made him feel. He hoped the skipper of the gunboat would buy it. He knew from his own experience as an officer that while one could push green shavetails and ensigns around, anyone who'd held his rank a little longer tended to push back.

As the boarding party went back over the side, Captain Gringo gave back the real skipper's hat. The older man heaved a long sigh and said, "All right, it worked, for now. I mean to weigh anchor before they come back for a rematch. Our next port of call will be Tehuantepec. I sure hope you boys have friends there. Because that's where you'll be going ashore."

Gaston came out from under the rug to join them as Captain Gringo said, "Let's give our friends here another few minutes. That navy launch is almost out of sight now."

The skipper started to say something. Gaston casually took out his six-inch blade and began to clean his fingernails with it as Captain Gringo put a hand inside his jacket and added, "Pretty pretty please?" So the skipper said he'd wait another five minutes, period.

They never got to discover just how he meant to weigh anchor without licking them both. Because it was less than five minutes before a dark lighter, lying low in the water, bumped alongside. Nobody came aboard. Someone in the lighter called out, in Spanish, "If anyone wishes for to go ashore, they had better move fast. We are not getting paid enough to spend the night out here!"

The skipper shouted orders in English to his crew and warned the men in the lighter that he'd shoot them if they tried to leave before he got rid of a couple of lunatics and their belongings. So a few minutes later Captain Gringo, Gaston, and their gear were on their way across the dark harbor with a Mexican crew not any friendlier than the guys who'd almost literally thrown them off the schooner.

Gaston asked the nearest sweep a polite question about their destination and was told, "We are not paid for to talk. We are paid for to take you ashore. The people we are delivering you to may wish for to gossip with you. They may not. If you don't like it, swim."

The lighter put in on a shingle beach beyond the last lights of the quay that less-secretive people tied up to. The men who'd brought them ashore dumped their bales and boxes on the sea-wet rocks and told them to get the hell out of their boat. Captain Gringo didn't see anyone else around. When he asked about that, the lighter skipper told him they wouldn't have put in there if there had been anyone waiting. He told his men to shove off. So they did, leaving the two soldiers of fortune and their gear to their own devices in the moonlight. Gaston sat on an ammo box and said, "The natives I met in North Africa with the Legion had better manners. Have you ever had the feeling you were not welcome, Dick?"

"Yeah. Don't light that smoke. Someone's coming."

Gaston got back to his feet and they both took out their revolvers and held them in the side pockets of their jackets as bare feet padded over the shingle toward them. As the strangers got closer, they turned out to be a gang of kids. The biggest one, no older than twelve, took off his straw sombrero and asked, "Do you need help with your luggage, señores?"

Captain Gringo replied, "Quién sabe? We would have to know where we were going before we decided, muchacho."

"I am called Gorrion. I know where you are going, señor."

"Would it be too much to ask you where, Gorrion?"

"Sí, señor. We are being paid for to take you and your luggage there, not to ask or answer questions."

"That sounds fair. Let's go, then."

Gorrion told the other kids to pick up the stuff as he told the two soldiers of fortune to follow him. He didn't offer to carry a thing, himself. Gaston muttered in English, "What a lovely child. Can you imagine what he'll be like by the time he's old enough to shave, Dick?"

Captain Gringo smiled thinly and said, "Rank has its privileges in any organization. They'd probably be acting nicer if they were out to screw us. But keep your eyes peeled and your hand in that pocket anyway."

"Merde alors, did you really think you had to tell me that? But let us look at the bright side. Since everyone we have met up to now insists on treating us so rudely, we should not feel guilty when we have to cross them double, hein?"

"Watch the mouth. Kids who carry things for tourists tend to pick up English fast."

If the punk in the lead had any idea what they thought of his manners, he didn't show it. Gorrion led them inland into a tangle of cabbage palmetto, then cut left along a dark dirt path toward the lights of the little fishing port. But before they got close enough to the lights to worry about them, Gorrion cut right along another byway, this one through prickly pear, and led them around the outskirts of town to the back door of a low rambling building. His followers placed the stuff they'd carried this far against the stucco wall on either side of the door. Then Gorrion snapped, "Vamanos, muchachos!" and they all scampered off into the darkness without another word.

The soldiers of fortune looked at each other. Captain Gringo said, "Dis must be de place. Cover me while I knock."

"I have a better idea. Let's run."

Captain Gringo ignored him and stepped over to knock on the door. It opened before he could, and a voice from the inner darkness said, "Entre por favor. We have been expecting you, Captain Gringo."

The voice sounded pleasant as well as feminine. But Captain Gringo asked, "Could we have some light on the subject, señorita? I mean no disrespect, but my mother told me never to walk into anything blind."

She laughed and struck a match as she said that her own mother had told her never to do a lot of things she'd done anyway. He believed her. She was a tough-looking little mutt with mixed Indian and Spanish features. She wouldn't have been bad-looking if she hadn't looked so hard and unkempt. She held up the match long enough to let him see that she wasn't pointing anything but her pelvis at him and that the room behind her was empty. Then she shook it out, saying, "Lights attract moths and other insects in this part of town. I am called Pilar. Did you bring the machine gun?"

He said he had. So she told him to get everything inside, for God's sake, and it only took the two men a few moments to do so. As they straightened up in the darkness, Pilar shut the door, bolted it, and struck another match to light a coal-oil lamp, saying, "Bueno. We should be safe here for the night. We will be leaving for the mountains in the morning."

Captain Gringo asked, "Where's here, and what do you mean when you say *we* in connection with the Sierra Madres, Pilar? Gaston and I learned our soldiering in armies that didn't march with adelitas much."

Gaston muttered, "Merde alors, speak for yourself!"

But since he said it in English, Pilar ignored Gaston and told Captain Gringo, "We are not adelitas, we are smugglers. Come, I shall introduce you to your other guide, Concepción."

She picked up the lamp and turned away toward another door. So they followed her, if only to avoid being left in the dark. In the next room an older and fatter mestiza who'd obviously heard their arrival was putting tin plates of refritos and tortillas on a crude table, painted blue of course. Pilar introduced her companion as Concepción and told them to sit down. So they did. Captain Gringo assumed it was about time he put his .38 back in its holster under his left armpit, so he did that, too. Pilar nodded approvingly and said she admired men who thought on their feet.

As she took her own seat, Concepción brought a pitcher of sangria to the table as well. As she sat down and dug in with no further ceremony, Captain Gringo said, "Well, you girls look tough enough to climb mountains with. But what about our stuff? We brought too much for four people to pack."

Pilar said, "I know. That is for why we have two mules. They are in what was once a spare bedroom, next to the room we left your things in. It is not safe to leave anything outside in this part of town."

"I asked you before just where we were, Pilar."

"I know. It is not important, since you shall never see this place again and, should you ever be picked up by los rurales, would not really have any need to give them this address. We have friends who watch the old dump when we are out of town. We are out of town a lot."

"I gathered as much, Pilar. How many smuggling runs have you girls made, so far?"

"Enough for to know the way. I know what you are thinking. You are thinking we do not look like border jumpers. That is one reason we have never been caught. It will be harder, this time. A party of two men and two women look like they are *going* somewhere, even when the men look like

Mexicans. Sombreros are no problem. But we are going to have to do something about those gringo linen suits.''

Concepción poured herself some sangria as she said, in a much softer voice, that she thought the stand that sold peon clothing at the village market would still be doing business, since it wasn't late.

Pilar shook her head and said, ''They are both too blanco for to pass as charcoal burners. I think it might be best for to disguise them as native Mexicans of some substance. We shall tell anyone we meet near the coast that we are going prospecting.''

Gaston asked what about people they met further inland, and she laughed harshly and said, ''Anyone who asks questions of strangers in the Sierra Madres is too crazy for to go on living. The idea is to look like a party too dangerous to attack without a good reason, and too poor to offer a good reason, eh?''

Gaston chuckled fondly and said, ''I am beginning to believe you lovely ladies do know your way around in these parts.'' He turned to Captain Gringo and added in English, ''What do you think, Dick?''

Captain Gringo said, ''Speak Spanish. We either trust one another or we don't.'' He turned back to Pilar and added, ''I think you girls must know the way, since you've made it back and forth more than once. If you know my nickname, you know a little about me, too. The company hired you as guides. They hired Gaston and me to head the expedition.''

She shrugged and replied, ''So?'' and he said, ''So we begin by cutting out all this street-gang *tu madre* nonsense. When I ask questions, even Gaston here answers them. If you're afraid we might turn you in, you don't know enough for us to bother taking you along. You girls, at best, are wanted for simple trespass and customs violations. The two of us are wanted for more grown-up shit. Is any of this getting through to you, or do I have to talk slower and move my hands a lot?"

Concepción giggled and murmured, "Ay, qué toro!"

But Pilar looked as sullen as ever as she answered, "I am used to being the boss here."

He said, "I noticed. I just took over, anyway. If you don't like it, say so, and we'll just be on our way."

She frowned and said, "Do not speak so estupido. You would never get through the Sierras without us. Besides, we have already taken the front money, and we are women of honor."

"I'm sure you are. I'm sure you want the final payment, too, and you won't get it until we get in and out with the insurance company's client. So let's talk about that. How many days will we be on the trail, Pilar?"

She shrugged and said, "Three or four. Maybe more. It depends on who else is using the trails. There is more than one route to follow, in places. We have found it wiser to go the long way around when we see campfire smoke ahead."

"That's the way I travel in Indian country, too. How bad *are* the local Indians, by the way?"

"Indians are not hard to deal with, when one has plenty of ammunition. Bandits are another matter. Bandits tend to have repeating rifles, too."

"I've noticed that. So tell me about the bandits. Are we likely to run into this Caballero Blanco everyone's so worried about?"

Pilar said. "Not on this side of the border. He is not exactly a bandit. He says he means to liberate Guatemala from the current junta and give schools and hospitals to the little people."

Captain Gringo grimaced and said, "Right. Meanwhile he

of course collects contributions to his cause at gunpoint. We've met his kind before. One of them's the president of Mexico at the moment. But we don't have to worry about high-minded Guatemalan rebels until we get to Guatemala. Which way is this market you girls mentioned? You're right about it being a good idea to pick up some charro outfits.''

Pilar protested, "Imposible! You can't go into town tonight!"

"I didn't ask your permission to go shopping, dammit. I asked you which way the market was!"

"It is due north, along the camino out front. But what if you get caught?''

"I'll be in a hell of a mess. Gaston, you stay here and mind the shop. I know your size and you can have any color charro outfit you want, as long as it's granite gray."

Gaston just chuckled as the tall American rose, put his hat back on, and headed for the door. Pilar started to rise, too. But Gaston said, "Don't try to stop him, querida. It's a waste of time. I think he is crazy, too. But that is the way he is. Would you girls like to play spin the bottle with me until he gets back, if he gets back?''

Captain Gringo didn't think he was acting crazy as he followed the dirt road into the lit-up center of town. He knew the insurance company had fixed the local if not the federale law, and the snippy navy jerk-off had told him a whole mess of other strangers were in town at the moment.

When he found his way to the open-air market he saw it was true. A pair of couples wearing the tropic kit of the new International Red Cross were gawking at the local color more obviously and less politely than an old Latin American hand like Captain Gringo thought prudent. The two women wore a sort of khaki nursing-sister's uniform. The men with them looked like they were on Safari in Darkest Africa, pith helmets and all. They were saved from being taken for a pair of Stanleys looking for Livingstone by their Red Cross armbands and their lack of weaponry. He'd heard the Red Cross didn't approve of packing guns. But you couldn't have it both ways, this deep in Mexico.

Most Mexicans were as polite to innocent-looking strangers as the next guy. But when you wanted to swagger and sneer around Mexican villagers, it was a good idea to do so with one hand resting on the grips of a serious-looking side arm.

None of the local natives seemed to give Captain Gringo more than a passing glance as he walked quietly among the market stalls. But the Red Cross workers were attracting murderous looks and silent curses as they tittered about, fingering goods and commenting on them in English without even nodding to the shabby barefoot merchants.

It wasn't Captain Gringo's problem. So he avoided them and any questions they might ask by cutting down a side aisle and asking an old woman selling fruit, politely, if she knew where they sold clothing. She told him where to go and he bought a papaya from her, gravely waiting for her to make change. Poor people could take an obvious tip the wrong way and they both knew he'd thanked her enough by buying one of her overripe papayas.

He got rid of it as soon as he was out of her sight, as she no doubt expected him to. He wondered how the hell she existed on the few sales she could possibly make.

He found another old woman selling vaquero gear and bought a pair of modest charro outfits trimmed with black braid instead of mock silver conchos. He knew how *she* survived. She charged too much for such an out-of-the-way village. But she was pleasant enough as she made his change, once she'd seen he was neither a haggler nor a cheapskate.

She asked politely if he was with the other Anglo strangers in her village. When he said he wasn't, she said, "Bueno. I would stay away from them if I were you, señor. *Far* away, if you are the peaceful young man I assume you to be."

He put the bundle under his left arm, leaving his gun hand free, as he smiled and asked casually, "Oh? Are those Red Cross people in trouble *already,* señora?"

She shrugged and replied, "It is not for me to say. But when a bleached-blond gringa points at a stand selling religious figures and laughs like a chicken, one tends to wonder about her continued good health. The figure she mocked was that of Santa Maria, madre de Dios! She seemed to find the costume of the Virgin more amusing than we do. If you are not with them, it would be wise to finish your shopping early."

The old woman put a finger to her cheek, pulled down a lower eyelid, and added, "Need I say more, señor?"

He shook his head, thanked her for her sage advice, and turned away. He knew the smartest thing to do right now would be to take the tip at face value and start making tracks. Like most adults of any race, the old market woman and probably most of the other merchants were trying to keep a lid on it, at least until closing time. But there were always clowns who had nothing better to do in any tough neighborhood, and beating up strangers was second only to bullfighting as the national sport of Mexico!

As he headed across the market to rejoin Gaston and the girls, he heard a distant female laugh. The old woman had been right. It did sound like a chicken trying to lay a square egg. But he didn't think the Red Cross girl was trying to lay an egg. The only egg in question was about to hit the fan any minute. So what in the hell was he doing here?

As he came to a cross aisle, he spotted a couple of obvious village toughs who were fortunately looking the other way, toward the source of the amused cackles. Captain Gringo moved on, slower, as he argued with himself. It wasn't his fight. It figured to be a mean one. The two Red Cross guys were unarmed and outnumbered. Worse, they didn't even know they were in trouble.

He came to another crossway as he heard the annoying cackle again. He sighed and turned down it. The dame was a dope. But she probably meant no real harm, and they'd both been too pretty, he recalled, to deserve the Mark of the Cow carved on their faces for the rest of their lives.

He saw he'd asked for even more trouble than expected when he spotted what was coming up the aisle between the stands to meet him. It was a three-man navy shore patrol, led by a burly CPO. All three were armed with pistols and billy clubs. All three were looking at him thoughtfully as he continued toward them. He didn't *want* to continue toward them, but he knew it would make them even more thoughtful if he turned and ran like hell. He could probably get away via some broken field running through the crowded marketplace. But he didn't want Uncle Sam even to guess that there was at least one obvious Anglo in town who didn't want to say howdy for some reason.

So, as he got within earshot, Captain Gringo nodded to the CPO and said, "I'm sure glad I ran into you guys. There's going to be a free-for-all."

The CPO replied, "That's what we heard. Some kid just ran up to us and said his mama sent him to tell us some white folks are in a jam."

Captain Gringo said, "He told you true. Follow me."

The CPO had gotten his stripes obeying the voice of command and Captain Gringo had learned to command pretty good a while back, leading a cavalry troop in Apache country. So the shore patrol fell in with him as he marched on the sound of the guns, or, in this case, chicken cackles. But, since the commanding stranger was still obviously dressed as a civilian, the CPO felt free to inquire where the hell they were going.

Captain Gringo said, "Some of those Red Cross workers we're supposed to be looking out for have been acting like tourists above and beyond the call of duty. The locals are fixing to jump them. Probably as they leave the market. But maybe sooner, if that silly dame doesn't shut up. Have you pulled this duty in a Latin port before, chief?"

"Yeah. I get the picture. Are you packing a gun, mister?"

"Of course. But we may be able to get everyone off the hook with a ruse. No time to explain. I see the intended prey ahead, in front of that hat stand. Just play along with me, chief. I know what I'm doing, I hope."

The Red Cross workers were now pestering the old man selling straw sombreros. At least, the big buck-toothed blonde was. The two men and the other girl, a little brunette, seemed sort of embarrassed as the blonde put a big sombrero on with another chicken laugh and asked them how she looked in it. The little brunette said, "Silly, Trixie. I wish you'd cut it out. I don't think the old man here shares your ideas of humor."

As Captain Gringo and the navy men moved in, the CPO murmured, "Oh boy, those greasers on the far side are moving to cut them off from the nearest exit!"

One of the other shore patrolmen added, "Don't look now, but there's another bunch edging in from behind us, chief!"

Captain Gringo said, "Pretend you don't notice. Here's

where I find out how much I really know about Mexican psychology.''

He marched up to the Red Cross workers, snatched the sombrero from the blonde's head, and placed it firmly back on the stand with the others as he shouted, ''So *you're* the silly bitch who dared to insult the mother of God!''

All four of the Red Cross workers stared at him, thunderstruck. He'd shouted in English because it would have been too obvious a ruse in Spanish. But, as he'd hoped, a native who spoke English laughed and translated his remarks to the crowd.

The blond gasped and said, ''What are you talking about! Who are you, anyway?''

Captain Gringo kept his voice loud enough for his volunteer translator as he snapped, ''Never mind who I am. You people are under arrest!''

The shore patrol was just as surprised, but smart enough to wait and see. So one of the Red Cross men got to shout, with a Dutch or German accent, ''Don't be ridiculous! We have done nothing. We are members of the International Red Cross!''

Captain Gringo roared, ''I don't care who you are, you son of a bitch! I'm still taking you in, and all four of you are going to be in prison until you're old and gray!''

The Red Cross workers gasped collectively and the little brunette, bless her, started to cry. The other man, who hadn't spoken, asked in French what was going on. The one who spoke English didn't answer him. He asked Captain Gringo what the charge was. The tall American said, ''Sacrilege. You poked fun at a figure of the Madonna and you're going to pay for it, you stupid bastard!''

The Red Cross man blinked in confusion and the big

blonde cackled weakly and said, "That's ridiculous! The Spanish Inquisition went out of business years ago!"

"This isn't Spain. It's los Estados Unidos de Mejico, and we're wasting time here. Chief, I want a guard on either side of these prisoners as we march them off to see the judge. Let's move it out!"

The CPO hesitated only a moment. He'd said he'd pulled this kind of duty before. He nodded and barked, "Simmons, secure the prisoners on the left. Ryan, you take the right flank. We'll take 'em to the brig for now. Let 'em sweat a bit before the judge sees them in the morning!"

A big, tough-looking Mexican who'd just joined the audience asked what was going on, in Spanish. A young tough who'd been thoughtfully cleaning his nails with an eight-inch blade laughed and told him, "The gringo policia are arresting them for sacrilege. They are going to prison for mocking the figure of Santa Maria."

"Es verdad? I did not know gringos were so religious."

"Neither did I. But even a *gringo* must believe in God, no? Julio understands their language. He says he thinks the four of them are in much trouble."

Captain Gringo didn't let on that he understood as, having waited until the shore patrolmen were in position, he shouted in English, "All right, prisoners, let's go. I warn you not to make a break for it when we get to the darker streets to the north, unless you want to be *shot!*"

It worked. The toughs blocking the nearest route out made way for them, grinning, as Captain Gringo and the navy men marched the so-called prisoners out of the market. One of them passed a truly dreadful remark at the two women, but since Captain Gringo didn't want them to know he spoke Spanish, he let it go. The blonde, at least, probably deserved it. And the sobbing little brunette didn't *know* they'd suggested she suck off the warden, so what the hell.

When it was safe to talk, the CPO laughed gleefully and told Captain Gringo, "I sure thought we were in for it back there. Are you secret service, mister?"

"If I told you, it wouldn't be a secret. Let's keep in formation a few more blocks in case anyone's keeping an eye on us."

"I get the picture, SS. But where are we going?"

It was a good question. So Captain Gringo stepped closer to his "prisoners" and told the English-speaking man, "Lead us to your own field headquarters. But don't look like you're leading us, right?"

"We're not about to go anywhere *else,* you maniac! Would someone please tell us what on earth is going on?"

Captain Gringo said, "You four were about to be jumped back there. We pretended to arrest you because most Mexicans would rather take a good beating than go to jail."

The little brunette gasped and said, "Oh, thank God! I thought we were really in trouble!"

He said, "You still could be, ma'am. The four of you had better not go into town again until your unit leaves. When would that be, by the way?"

The now subdued blonde said, "We're not sure. Our leaders are having trouble getting guides. We assumed it would be easy. But when we told the people here we wanted to go up into the Sierra Madres, nobody seemed to want the job."

Captain Gringo nodded but didn't answer as he digested that. The man who spoke English was explaining the situation in French to the other Red Cross guy, who laughed a lot like Gaston did when he got the whole picture. The little brunette told Captain Gringo she was ever so grateful and had no idea

how she'd ever repay him for his quick-witted kindness.
Captain Gringo just smiled at her, too. He had a couple of
things in mind, if he could manage to work out this new
development the way he meant to try.

He couldn't. When they all got to the posada the Red Cross
was using as temporary field headquarters, the navy shore
patrol parted in friendly fashion to go looking for more
trouble. Captain Gringo went inside with the four workers
he'd rescued, and smoked a third of a cigar by the time it had
all been explained and he'd been properly thanked by the
expedition commander, an old goat with a Swiss accent who
held court at a corner table in the cantina but didn't offer
anything but coffee to drink. His name was Fitzke. Herr
Doktor Fitzke, to hear him tell it.

Captain Gringo let Fitzke run down before he said, "I'll be
leaving for the Sierra Madres and the Guatemalan high
country in the morning, doc. I've got native guides, a
sidekick who shoots pretty good, and plenty of stuff to shoot.
We'd be willing to join your party, if you like."

Fitzke pursed his lips and said, "Impossible. The International Red Cross is not allowed to carry weapons."

Captain Gringo frowned and said, "Are you serious, doc?
That's wild and woolly country we're talking about. It's not
safe up there in the Sierra Madres even *with* guns. The snakes
are bad enough. The locals would never forgive themselves if
they let food, supplies, and medicine, along with a mess of
real live women, pass through without at least making the old
college try."

"Nonetheless, the International Red Cross is bound to

abide by its charter, Mein Herr. We are not a military organization. We are forbidden to behave as one.''

''Sir, the people where you're going never heard of the International Red Cross. A lot of them don't even speak Spanish. Whoever wrote those rules for you never could have had the Sierra Madres in mind!''

The old goat just shrugged and smiled smugly. Captain Gringo said, ''All right, there's still some safety in numbers, and my friends and I do have guns. Would it be against your charter if we just came along for laughs? We won't charge you a centavo, and I understand you can't get anyone else to guide you.''

Fitzke shook his head and said, ''As a matter of fact, I managed to hire two Mexican guides just this evening. So we won't need your, ah, services, Mein Herr.''

Captain Gringo frowned and asked, ''Have you told your Mexicans that they don't get to bring any guns along, doc?''

''Of course. Naturally, they agreed.''

''You mean naturally they're crazy or don't know the Sierra Madres worth a damn, doc! The damned *rurales* are afraid to wander around up there, and they come with Winchesters and Colt .45s they practice a lot with! I'd like to see these so-called guides of yours.''

''I'm afraid that is impossible, Mein Herr. They are not here. They have gone to make preparations for the trip and will be joining us in the morning. But what could you possibly want with them? I thought you already had your own guides, Mein Herr.''

Captain Gringo shook his head wearily and said, ''I didn't want to swipe them, I assure you. I just wanted to see if they were both real Mexicans.''

''What else would they be, Swedes?''

''They sure as hell can't be local natives, doc. Everyone in this part of Mexico knows you don't take women and other goodies worth fighting for into the high scrub without even a BB gun! How many people are we talking about, anyway?''

Fitzke sniffed and said, ''There are thirty male field workers and ten nursing sisters in this relief expedition, if it's any of your business. Why?''

Captain Gringo picked up his bundle, got to his feet, and said, ''There's a chance that big a bunch may look like too big a boo for the average raiding party. But the odds against you getting through are still lousy, even if your dopey guides know the way. I'm still willing to help. But if I'm wasting my breath, just say so and I'll be on my way, doc.''

Fitzke said he was. So he left, muttering under his breath. He'd have never saved four of the idiots from the local villagers had he known they all meant to be murdered by bandits anyway.

He had to pass through the market again to get back to Pilar's hideout. So on the way he stopped at another stall and picked up three old Spencer repeating rifles, with ammo to fit the bore. He would have bought more, had the gunsmith had any in stock. But, as it was, he was packing quite a load when he got back to Pilar's.

The front door was locked. He kicked it a few times and at last Pilar got around to letting him in. She frowned at the extra guns as he placed them on the table. She asked who they were for and he said, ''I'm not sure. We may make some converts along the way. Where's Gaston?''

''In bed with Concepción. He asked me to join them, but I don't go in for kid games.''

''Oh? What sort of games *do* you go in for, Pilar?''

She shrugged and said, ''I'll sleep with you, if you like. It's up to you. It's only fair to warn you I am an old-fashioned girl. I only like for to fuck.''

He laughed and said he admired old-fashioned girls. He hadn't been thinking along those lines until just now. He wondered why, as Pilar picked up the lantern and led him into another room. She looked a lot softer from behind and he hadn't had a woman since that wild night with the twins back in Costa Rica.

Pilar had fixed up her own bleak little room with a sleeping pallet on the floor in one corner and a plaster Madonna in a corner niche. A votive candle was already burning in front of the little santa. So Pilar blew out her lamp and placed it on the floor near the door as she closed and bolted it. Even by soft candlelight she looked tough as hell.

But as she slipped off her peon blouse, exposing her firm breasts, he could see she wasn't a surly teen-aged boy with long black hair after all. She said, "Get in bed. I'll join you in a moment."

That sounded reasonable. So he shucked his hat and jacket and sat on the pallet to finish undressing as Pilar, with no trace of shyness, unfastened her skirt, let it fall, and stepped out of it stark naked in the candlelight. She wasn't built like a teen-aged boy below the waist, either, and Captain Gringo was already rising to the occasion as she stood there with her hands on her firm hips to ask him, "Well, do you think I'm worth the time and effort, Captain Gringo?"

He said, "Call me Dick, and get over here muy pronto, querida!"

She smiled thinly and said, "Sí, sí, un momento," as she turned from him to face the plaster Madonna and dropped to her knees before it with her naked back to him. He watched, bemused, as Pilar offered a silent prayer, or perhaps a lewd wink, to the garishly painted little figure. Then she crossed herself, rose, dusted off her bare knees, and came to join him as he asked with a puzzled frown if she always said her prayers like a good little girl before she went to bed with a man.

She said, "I pray every night before I go to sleep, whether I have company or not." Then she shoved him down roughly, forked a leg over his supine flesh, and grabbed his erection to guide it in as she impaled herself on him.

He hissed, "Jeeez!" as her wet warmth reminded him how long indeed it had been since he'd been in such nice surroundings. She was tight as well as hot, but didn't subject him to the usual maidenly gasp as she took it to the hilt and proceeded to screw him, very nicely, while she calmly observed, "You have a nice cock. I'm glad. We are going to be spending many nights on the trail together and I hate to play with myself, don't you?"

He chuckled and said, "I like this a lot better than my hand. Let me get on top, querida."

She moved faster, contracting skillfully, and replied, "Not yet. I like for to be in command. Don't you like what I am doing, Deek?"

"Very much. But I'd like it better if I was in charge."

She hitched her bare heels forward to throw her weight on them as she began to move up and down in long, teasing strokes, saying, "In my own bed, *I* am the boss, Deek. Ah, I felt that. But you can't take it out until *I* come, too!"

He didn't answer. He just lay there letting her milk the last drops of his unexpected but not at all unpleasant first ejaculation. Her brown skin was shiny with sweat as she tried to move even faster with her full weight on her smooth but powerful legs. He knew for sure, now, that old Pilar was used to hiking over mountains a lot. But he could tell she was starting to tire, too. So he simply reached up, pulled her heaving slippery breasts down aginst his chest, and rolled over with it still inside her as she protested, "No! I wished for to come on *top!*"

He hooked an elbow under each of her slippery brown knees and spread her thighs wider as he proceeded to pound her hard. With her tailbone against the firm floor pallet it was easy to hit bottom with every stroke, and she forgot her street-punk act as she gasped and said, "Madre de Dios! What do you think I am, a bottomless pit! You are too big for to do it to me that way. You are hurting me and . . . Ay caramba! It feels so good and I am, oh, Jesus, Maria, y José, I am cominggggg!"

That made two of them. So Captain Gringo stopped to let it soak as they swapped spit and cooing noises while her insides rippled like warm wet velvet on his shaft. When they came up for air, Pilar said, "That was not fair. How was I to know you carried such a concealed weapon?"

"Have we settled it about who's the boss of this expedition, Pilar?"

She laughed and asked, "Is this an expedition? It feels like fucking. But, bueno, I do not mind taking orders from a man, if he is a real man, and if you were any more real I would need a doctor right now! Could we rest a moment, querido? Doing this with you takes a little getting used to!"

He kissed her, dismounted, and reached for his shirt to fish out a claro and a light. As they cuddled together after he'd lit up, Pilar shared the cigar with him, commenting on the good tobacco. She smoked like a tough little mutt, too. But now that they'd gotten to know each other a little better, she was feminine enough to ask him about the extra guns. He told her about the Red Cross expedition's odd views on weaponry and she agreed that they were trying to commit suicide. But she still didn't see how the old Spencers could possibly help.

He said, "We'll let them start ahead of us. We'll follow just out of sight behind them. Do you want to make an educated guess about what has to happen next?"

She took a puff on the claro, handed it back to him with a frown, and said, "It is not a guess. It is a certainty that they will walk into an ambush within a day or so. But why should we care, Deek? We are not Red Cross workers."

He took a drag and said, "No, but we still have to get where they're going. If they're out front, they'll run into trouble before we can, see?"

"Better them than us. But for why do we need extra weapons? Concepción and I have our own and you two men have pistols, rifles, and that machine gun as well, no?"

"Call me a soft-hearted slob. But if those Red Cross guys live long enough, some of them may know how to shoot. Four old rifles spread among forty people won't help much, but it's better than nothing."

"Ah, you mean to *sell* them the repeaters when they see the light?"

"We'll work something out. It depends on how many of 'em are left to see anything. What are the odds on the guys in the Sierra Madres jumping a party that size, not knowing they don't have guns, Pilar?"

She shrugged and said, "Quién sabe? Los Indios may not attack them if their guides are smart enough to steer them clear of any villages or sacred places. The guerrillas have better weapons, but taking on thirty men who *could* be armed is not an adventure to consider lightly. They may make it through the smaller bands. If El Caballero Blanco and his hombres are between here and the cut-off first rescue party, the second one is as good as done for."

"The White Knight doesn't scare easy?"

"El Caballero Blanco is in the habit of fighting the Guatemalan army regularly, and they have tried for to kill him with field artillery! Thirty men in any kind of uniform would be just what El Caballero Blanco would desire for a light supper. The ten women, of course, would make a good dessert!''

"Let's hope nobody runs into a serious rebel band, then. Shall we get some sleep, or are you game for some dessert, too?''

She asked him if he was kidding. So he laughed and started to snuff out the claro on the dirt floor. She took it from him and said, "Wait, do not put it out. I wish to take a few more drags on it.''

He thought she meant she wanted to puff it with her mouth some more. She didn't. As he reclined on one elbow to watch, bemused, Pilar spread her thighs and lay on her back to shove the wet, unlit end of the claro up her love box, and, sure enough, she could puff it pretty good *that* way, too.

As he watched the glowing tip winking like a red firefly on the end of her unusually improvised dildo, he said mildly, "You told me you didn't go in for crazy sex, querida.''

She said, "I am not doing this for to show off. The smoke makes me more sensitive inside, see?''

"I see indeed, and it's giving me another hard-on, for some dumb reason. Aren't you already, ah, tenderized enough in there, doll box?''

She giggled and said, "It tickles and teases and I know you have already come twice. So if I am to arouse you again I must add spice to my tamale, no?''

It was teasing him, too, just watching, as he considered the smooth internal muscles expanding and contracting on that big cigar. It was enough to make a guy feel jealous. He said, "I don't know if you've noticed, querida, but I'm already about as hard as a guy can get. Let's cut this smoking in bed and do it right.''

She rolled her head on the pillow, glanced down, and said, "Oh, you *do* seem to be hot again, no?''

"That's what I just said. Take that dumb thing out and let me get in again."

She laughed, started to withdraw the claro, then moved it in and out of herself experimentally as she said, "Oh, this feels so strange."

"It looks strange, too. Do you always jerk yourself off when there's a perfectly good real thing at your disposal?"

She started doing it faster as she replied, "No. This is the first time I've tried this, with a man watching. It is giving me a very strange thrill. I wonder what it would feel like if I went all the way with it."

He grimaced and said, "Jesus, this is the first time I've ever had a fucking cigar steal my girl."

She said, "Lie back down, Deek. I wish for to try something." He shrugged and lay back, muttering, "Whatever Gaston and Concepción are doing next door has to make more sense."

Then he closed his eyes and hissed in pleasure as she rolled over onto her hands and knees to go down on him as she went on dildoing herself with the claro. For a girl who said she was old-fashioned, Pilar sure sucked like an old pro, and this was sure an easier way to come than most, so what the hell.

It was just as well that he was semisated, given the skillful way she offered head. He knew he'd have come by now if she'd *started* this freaky way. She began to move on her knees to aim her brown rump at the head of the pallet, next to his. He didn't know about that. He could be as good a sport as the next guy with a reasonably clean lady he knew better. But the tough little mestiza had been a bit gamy even before she was sweated up and filled with his and who knew who else's love juice.

But that wasn't what she wanted. She spit him out just long enough to say, "Help me with the cigar, por favor!" So, as she inhaled again with her mouth, he laughed and took hold of the claro to slide it in and out of her while he fingered her wet clit with the other hand. That did it for her. She sobbed, swallowed his shaft all the way, and blew smoke out her vagina. He could tell from the vibrations of the now ruined-for-good cigar that she was coming, hard.

He did, too, deep in Pilar's throat. But, wanting to finish right, before it went soft on him, he withdrew the cigar, threw it away, and shoved her forward to roll over and mount her from behind. And she was right about smoked meat having a tang all its own. It flashed hot and cold as he shoved it in and out of her while she beat the straw-filled pallet with her fists and sobbed that she'd never had it so good before.

He knew she was probably full of shit as well as his excited organ grinder. Dames knew they were expected to tell guys things like that no matter how many times they'd come with others or, in Pilar's case, probably anything that would fit. But he knew she wasn't faking when she came again and clamped down so hard that she popped him out as he was on the back stroke, almost there. He swore, fumbled it back between the slippery brown cheeks of her rollicking rump, and thrust home hard all the way. She gasped and arched her back to shove her brown cheeks up against him as he realized his error and said, "Oops, sorry, thought this was the other hole."

"Do it, do it, do it!" she said, sobbing. So he finished that way in less than ten strokes and collapsed on her soft brown back, saying, "I hope I didn't hurt you, querida."

She murmured, "You did, a little, but I've always wondered what it would feel like back there. Don't move. It doesn't hurt now. But, madre de Dios, it feels so *big* in there."

He knew she was shitting him about her shit hole's virginity, too. No dame liked it this way unless she'd done it a few times with someone or something. From the skilled way she rippled *those* internal muscles, he suspected a banana or perhaps a burro had had her this way ahead of him. He wondered why a dame who looked so tough and made love so wildly felt the need to pretend it was all so new to her. Maybe she was just a compulsive liar. *That* was something to think about, when a dame was about to lead you into other new territory where a fib could cost a guy his life!

But he put the vague suspicion aside for the moment when Pilar purred, "You can start moving now, querido."

"You're sure you want to do it some more this way, doll box? I don't want to hurt you and I don't see what you're getting out of it."

She arched her spine teasingly and said, "It does not hurt. It feels most dirty and romantico at the same time, and that is what I am getting out of it. *Do* it, Deek! Fuck me in the ass, muy toro, and make me come this way, too!"

So he did, and she did. By the time they fell asleep in each other's arms, he was sort of looking forward to a week or so on the trail with this tough little mutt.

Since they wouldn't be leaving as early as planned, the girls cooked a warm breakfast the next morning as the soldiers of fortune regarded each other wryly across the table. They were both dressed like Mexican vaqueros and Gaston looked like he'd had a hard night, too. But both the fat Concepción and little Pilar seemed to glow as they busied themselves to take care of their newfound friends' other appetites. It wasn't polite to compare notes on pussy in front of ladies, so Captain Gringo brought Gaston up-to-date on the

Red Cross team and his plan to use them as advance scouts, with or without their knowledge or desire. Gaston said it was the smartest suggestion he'd made up to now and that it could only be topped by just tossing in the towel and running like hell.

Captain Gringo said that aside from being a breach of contract, it could wind up being more dangerous, in the end. He said, "We know what's ahead of us in the Sierra Madres. The girls will get us in, and nobody's after us in Guatemala right now."

Gaston said, "Oui, but once we get *in,* we must get *out,* and with at least one extra bit of baggage. This species of Red Cross girl the company is so worried about may not get along with your Pilar, if she is at all attractive, hein?"

"Oh, shit, we're not going in to *screw* her. We're going in to *rescue* her, you dope!"

"True. But where in the fine print does it say you have to be *rude* to her, Dick? I was hoping you might be able to persuade her to come with us with your usual charm. I see, this morning, that you have forfeited that advantage. Assuming, of course, you intend to use the same guides on the return trip."

They were speaking English. But one never knew. So Captain Gringo said, "Let's not discuss business at the table. We have to find Miss Swann alive and well before we can ask her about her sex life."

"What if she is not alive when we arrive, Dick? No word has been heard of that first Red Cross team since the volcanic indigestion cut them off up there."

"I wish you hadn't asked that. If they've all been cooked or killed by anything else, we're shit out of luck, of course. But we're not going to find out sitting here. What time is it?"

"Six-thirty, why?"

"Sunrise was at six. The Red Cross bunch will probably screw around awhile, but Fitzke said they were pushing off this morning. So let's give 'em another hour. We'll be moving faster, once we're moving. So if we're giving them a real lead, it still evens out."

The girls joined them at the table, and as they all dug in, Pilar asked what they were talking about. Captain Gringo explained about letting the other party get a good lead and Pilar said, "I do not like it. We usually slip out of town before daybreak, Deek."

He said, "I know. But they're not smugglers. They're greenhorns."

"What if we are stopped by curious law officers, Deek?"

"We tell them we're going out to gather firewood or something. You girls aren't combining business with pleasure this trip, are you?"

Pilar looked away and asked, "Whatever do you mean, querido?"

He grimaced and said, "Oh boy, I might have known. How much silver are you taking over the border with you, doll box?"

"Only a little. Just a few ingots. Is it important, Deek?"

"Only if we run into rurales, I suppose. We'll probably have to shoot it out with the pricks anyway. But let's not deal any more cards from the bottom, Pilar. Are you sure the silver's the only thing you were holding out on?"

She pouted and said, "I did not hold anything out on you, querido. When you asked about it, I told you about it, no?"

"I guess so. Who are we smuggling silver to, if the road to the Guatemalan lowlands is cut off?"

She looked away with a stubborn set to her jaw. He nodded and said, "Right. You did mention El Caballero Blanco in admiring terms last night. Okay. So we don't have to worry about his band, and you say the other bands are small and sneaky. I want you to listen carefully before you fib to me again, Pilar. Are you listening like a good little girl?''

She nodded, and he said, ''Numero uno, neither the company we're working for nor Gaston and I give a damn about the political situation in Guatemala. You know we're both wanted by the law. So we couldn't betray your White Knight if we wanted to. Agreed?''

She nodded again, and he said, ''Numero segundo, your pal El Caballero Blanco must like money or you wouldn't be smuggling it to him. He must know some Guatemalan trails that aren't on any map or he wouldn't be in a position to spend any dinero he gets from anyone. Do you think we could make a deal with him?''

She frowned and said, ''El Caballero Blanco does not like Anglos, Deek.''

He said, ''That's not what I asked. Nobody likes us as much as we like ourselves. But United Fruit still buys all the bananas they want down this way. We're talking cold cash, not popularity. You know the mission. You know we don't get the final payment until we get that overinsured Red Cross girl out alive and well. If Guatemalan rebels, wild Indians, or the man in the moon is willing to help us get her out, I'm willing to cut them in on the action.''

Gaston frowned and growled, ''Merde alors, we are talking about *my* money, too, Dick!''

Captain Gringo switched to English as he muttered, ''Upshay utshay, you asshole. A hundred bucks is a lot of money down here and that's all we're talking about.''

Pilar asked what Gaston was bitching about. Captain Gringo smiled reassuringly and said, ''Por nada. He's just a worrier. I just told him I was sure El Caballero Blanco was a sensible hombre. How do we go about contacting him, Pilar?''

She shrugged and said, ''Quién sabe? We are to deliver the silver to some friends of his in Guatemala. We may not meet him at all. This could be a good thing for you two, querido. When I tell you he does not like Anglos, I do not mean he is *undecided* about them! He has proclaimed more than once that Yanqui imperialists are the curse of Central America.''

''Do you think he'd overlook our past misdeeds for a hundred of our dollars or more? How much were you girls promised to get along so well with us, by the way?''

Pilar didn't answer, but Concepción said, ''Oh, we are each to get two hundred Yanqui dollars, once we finish this job, Deek.''

The soldiers of fortune exchanged glances. Gaston nodded and said, ''Mon Dieu, the company must think you girls are good if they are willing to pay so well for your services, hein?''

Captain Gringo kicked him under the table and said, ''Finish your breakfast. We've still got to lash our gear to a pack saddle.''

He turned back to Pilar and said, ''Since you don't seem ready to answer my question yet, I won't press you to right now, querida. But think about it. Talk it over with Concepción here, in private if you like.''

He finished his coffee, stood up, and told Gaston, ''I'll be with the mules, if you ever finish stuffing yourself.''

He left the kitchen. Gaston was smart enough to chase after him before the girls, who'd started later, could finish and join them.

The two Spanish mules tethered in what was supposed to be a guest room for people had shit all over the floor and one of them dropped another couple of turds nervously as they rolled their eyes at the strangers. Captain Gringo saw that one pack saddle in a wall niche had already been laden with the girls' trail gear. He picked up a bare one and with it moved toward the more constipated mule, saying softly, "Easy, boy. I'm willing to be friends if you are."

Gaston said, "Watch it, Dick. That one's a *biter!*"

Captain Gringo answered, "Never tell an old army man about mules. The other one's a kicker and bucker. I'd rather risk a bite on the ass than our gear scattered all along the dusty trail. Would you get our stuff from the next room while I saddle this son of a bitch? Leave the machine gun for last. I want it on top."

"Merde alors, now who's telling an old hound how to sniff trees?" snorted Gaston, leaving to get their gear while the tall American made friends with his transportation.

The mule didn't want to make friends. He sidestepped the pack-saddle pad and, as Captain Gringo held his rope halter, tried to bite his hand off.

It didn't work. Captain Gringo punched its muzzle, hard, and said soothingly, "You didn't really want to do that, did you?" Then he twisted the nose noose painfully tight and added as gently, "I'm putting the pad on now, mule. You don't get to breathe again until I do."

The mule got the message. Like those of both its horse and donkey ancestors, the mule's mouth and nasal passages were not connected. So it could only inhale through its nostrils, which made a head cold fatal to its species, and made it easier to control than it wanted to be, when a man understood basic equine anatomy. The mule stood still as Captain Gringo put on the pad, let it take a breath, and then saddled and cinched with no further argument.

Gaston staggered in with a lazy-man's load and helped him lash the bottom layer to the pack saddle. The mule noticed that Gaston was smaller than the one he'd given up on, for now, and tried to bite the little Frenchman, who grabbed its muzzle and said, "Surely you jest!" and bit it savagely on one ear, drawing blood as the mule tried to protest but couldn't, with Gaston's fingers up its nose. Captain Gringo said, "Hold him. I'll get the next load."

He brought their sleeping rolls in from the next room and lashed them to the mule. Then he went back for the ammo and, last of all, the machine gun. He lashed that, wrapped in a tarp of course, with the muzzle braced over the rear fork and the breech nestled by the forward one. Gaston offered him the harness rope and said, "Eh bien, while there is time, let us see how much silver they are smuggling, non?"

Captain Gringo said, "Non. Don't mess with their pack. It's not going to be easy to get to if Pilar smuggles as good as she does other things, and they'll be in here any minute."

Gaston shrugged, then winked and said, "The fat one is a très formidable lay too. So I'll forgive you, this time, for getting the pretty one."

Captain Gringo didn't answer, which was just as well. The two girls came in to join them. Pilar frowned at what they'd just done and said, "Just a moment, Deek. That was the mule *we* intended to use!"

He said, "I figured he was the best one, too. We've got a much heavier load, Pilar. Old buck there won't get us in as much trouble scraping your pack off on a tree as he would ours. If you lose your sleeping roll, don't worry. I'm sure we can work something out."

Pilar pouted and said, "His name is Eduardo, even if he is a bucker. This is most unjust. Both these mules are mine, and you have taken Roberto, my favorite! It is true Roberto bites, a little, but he is steadier on the trail."

Captain Gringo nodded and said, "That's what I just said. You'd better load your Eduardo with your pack saddle if you're going with us today, muchachas. It's getting late and we don't want that Red Cross too far out ahead of us."

So they did it, bitching all the while, and a short time later they were all on their way east, toward the foothills of the Sierra Madres.

To get there, they had to get out of the village first, and that was a bit more complicated than expected. Gaston, walking ahead as Captain Gringo led the lead mule, spotted the shore patrol first and hissed, "Sacre species of triple-thumbed toads! What are those très adorable sailor boys doing in the native quarter at such an ungodly hour?"

Captain Gringo said, "Let's ask them. Drop back and let me do the talking."

Gaston started to argue, but didn't. He could see it would look worse if they tried to avoid the patrol at this late date. The navy men had stopped in the shade of a live oak and were regarding the two men, two women, and two mules with undisguised curiosity. So far they hadn't drawn their pistols. Hoping to keep things that way, Captain Gringo stepped up the pace to approach them with a friendly smile as he asked in English, "Have you guys seen that Red Cross team this morning?"

The petty officer in command replied, "They left town about half an hour ago. Who wants to know?"

Captain Gringo moved closer, still smiling, as he tried to think up an answer they might buy. The petty officer's hand was on his pistol grips now. So the taller American kept both his hands in very plain view as he said, "We got a late start and we're trying to catch up with the column."

"That's not what I asked you, mister. Who the hell are you and do you have any papers to prove it?"

Captain Gringo said, "Sure," as he put a hand inside his charro jacket, hoping their mothers had never told them about shoulder holsters. But the day was saved when one of the junior members of the patrol took another look at Captain Gringo, grinned, and said, "Hey, I know *you*. I was with Chief Wilcox at the market last night. How come you're in Mex duds this morning?"

Captain Gringo didn't answer and the shore patrolman said, "Oh, right, stupid question."

The petty officer turned to the patrolman who'd met Captain Gringo before and growled, "You know this guy, Mason?"

"Sure. He's secret service. Chief Wilcox said so."

Captain Gringo sighed and said, "He's got a big mouth, too. How in hell am I supposed to keep secrets if the navy keeps blabbing about my mission to everyone?"

The new patrol leader laughed and said, "Don't get your shit hot, SS. We're on your side. Uncle has you watching them Red Cross jerk-offs for some reason, right?"

"I'm not supposed to tell."

"Shit, you don't have to. Most of them are damned furriners and the Mex government's being a pain in the ass about it, too. Is there anything we can do to help, SS?"

Captain Gringo laughed easily, said there wasn't, as he thanked them just the same, and they all parted company alive and well.

Gaston murmured, "Merde alors, that was close, and we have yet to reach the city limits of this très petite village!"

Captain Gringo said, "So pick 'em up and lay 'em down, but don't look back!"

"There you go telling your teacher how it's done again,

Dick. How on earth did you sell that très strange story to them, anyway?''

"It's a long story. Suffice it to say, everybody likes to look smarter than he really is. Slow down. I didn't mean you should hop, skip, and jump when I said to keep moving. If we don't want to catch up with that column, we'd better take it easy. A long column always moves slower on the march, even when it's all male.''

"There you go again, you fucking species of cavalry trooper. If we walk too slow, those adorable sailors we just passed might wonder just how serious we are about catching up, non?''

"Non. They're trained pros and they think we're shadowing the Red Cross for Uncle Sam, see?''

Gaston laughed and said, "Great minds run in the same channels, then, since that is exactly what we are doing. Ah, oui, regardez that fresh mule dropping in the dust ahead.''

"I just did. Flies haven't found it yet. That means they're less than half an hour ahead of us. But we'd better not call a trail break until we're out of town.''

They plodded on as the sun rose higher and the dust got hotter. Then, when they came to a banana grove by the side of the road, Captain Gringo led the way in, made sure that, as he'd assumed, nobody was working the unripe bananas, and tethered the mule to a stalk as he announced, "We'll shade here for at least a couple of hours. I hope. Pilar, you know this neck of the woods. Are we likely to have company here this morning?''

Pilar shook her head and said, "I do not think so. These bananas belong to old Tio Renaldo and he is a lazy drunk even when it is time for to pick them. But I do not think we had better take our clothes off while we fuck, just in case.''

Captain Gringo laughed and said, "We've got too much

ground to cover to tear off a piece every time we take a break, querida. Haven't you ever heard of just *resting?*"

He flopped to the weedy grass in the moist shade to recline on one elbow as Pilar flopped down beside him, saying, "You said we would be here two hours. How much rest does anyone need, Deek? It is too early for to eat again, and we have not walked far enough for to be tired. Are you cross with me because we argued about the mules?"

He said he wasn't. So she said, "Bueno," and hoisted her dark peon skirt up around her naked hips as she lay back and spread her brown thighs. He said, "For God's sake, it's broad daylight and we're not alone, you know!"

She said, "Yes, we are. Gaston and Concepción just went for a walk among the bananas, hand in hand. I do not think they went for to pick bananas, do you?"

He looked around, saw she was right, and said, "Just the same, some damned body has to watch the mules and that road over there, and I'm not worth a damn at that with my pants down."

"Just unbutton your fly, then. I will not mind. Those new pants look smooth."

"They are. They're clean, too. I mean to keep them that way for now, and besides, I'm not worried about the mechanics involved. I just can't guard our lives and supplies and screw at the same time. Can't you wait until tonight, for Pete's sake?"

She said, "Tonight may never come, and I am hot *now!* If you will not fuck me, I shall have to satisfy myself some other way."

He laughed and told her to be his guest. He was only kidding, but Pilar rolled to her feet, reached up into the nearest banana tree, and selected a green banana. A big one. Then, as he watched, bemused, the tough little mutt dropped down to the grass again and proceeded to fornicate with the local vegetation. It looked dirty as hell. So why was it giving him a hard-on to watch?

He knew if he watched her slide that big green substitute in and out of that hot little snatch much longer he was going to get jealous and change his mind. So he got to his own feet and moved over to check the cinches on the mules or something. The mules were fine. They liked it in the shade, eating weeds, and Eduardo's half-assed attempt to kick him missed by a mile and was only in fun. He looked back. Pilar had that banana going in and out as if she were churning butter inside her. Her eyes were closed and she rolled her dark head from side to side as she moved her hips in passion, mockery, or both. He grimaced and walked closer to the road. He wasn't expecting to see anyone coming along it from either direction. So he was more than a little surprised when he did.

Two dozen armed and dangerous-looking men were riding west toward the seaport at a bone-jarring but mile-eating steady trot. Like Captain Gringo and Gaston, they were dressed in gray charro outfits. But they were not vaqueros or anything else as human. They were rurales, and los rurales didn't ride in such big bunches unless they were on the trail of somebody El Presidente Diaz really wanted a *lot!*

Captain Gringo knew he was high on their list as he faded back through the bananas, drawing his .38 as he crawfished. There was no way in hell he was about to stop twenty-four homicidal maniacs with five bullets. But taking at least five of the pricks with him beat any higher hopes he might have if they failed to just ride by!

He could no longer see the dusty road now, but from the steady sound of hoofbeats it didn't seem they were going to stop to pick bananas, Lord be praised.

He made it back to the mules and cut around to start unlashing the machine gun as Pilar stopped jerking off long enough to ask what was going on, in a too-loud voice. He snapped, ''Rurales! Keep still!''

She didn't. She wailed, ''Oh, my God! Save me! Save me!''

He cursed, spun around, and took a running dive at her to clap a hand over her mouth and hiss, ''Jesus, Pilar! Have you gone nuts?''

She stared wild-eyed and struggled with him as he soothed, ''Easy. Easy. They seem to be riding on. Here, let me give you a hand with that banana.''

He removed his hand from her mouth and took the free end of the green banana firmly in hand to dildo her with it some more as he said, ''That's why I didn't want the real thing in you just now. Nobody thinks too straight when they're excited, But you sure get excited a lot, for a girl who's supposed to be used to playing hide-and-seek with the law!''

She spread her brown thighs wider and put a hand on the back of his wrist to help as she replied, ''I am used to ducking customs agents. But, madre de Dios, los rurales are not supposed to patrol these parts. Some evil person back in the village must have betrayed us! Ah, could you do that a little faster, querido?''

He could and he did, as he shook his head and said, ''They could be after almost anyone who doesn't admire El Presidente Diaz, and there's a lot of that going around in Mexico these days. I didn't notice a telegraph wire along the road we took out of town. *Is* there a telegraph Pilar?''

She answered only with a groan as Gaston came in view through the banana stalks, buttoning his pants. Gaston asked why he'd just heard a woman scream. Then he saw what they were doing and asked, ''Is that any way to treat a lady, Dick?

Move over and let a *man* do it *right* if you're not in the mood, hein?''

Captain Gringo let go of the banana, got to his feet, and put away the gun in his other hand as he told Gaston, ''Just trying to calm her nerves. A mess of rurales just rode by. I *think* they rode by. But just thinking isn't good enough when there are rurales anywhere near you. Screw her or something while I man the Maxim. But don't let her yell anymore!''

He moved back to the mules and finished unlashing the machine gun. He armed it and stepped clear of the mules with the Maxim braced on one hip, trained on the out-of-sight road. He strained his ears for at least a million years and all he heard was a greenfinch tweeting in the tree above him. He flinched when he heard a snapping twig behind him. But it was only Gaston coming to join him, pistol drawn, and observing, ''She seems to prefer fruit to older men. I don't think she'll scream again. I told her we'd kill her if she did. Shall I go get Concepción?''

The taller American said, ''Yeah. Tell her to get dressed, while you're at it. We'd better move the girls and mules farther back among the bananas. I'll cover your withdrawal from here with the Maxim.''

''Merci. Mais just what is our line of retreat, Dick? Concepción and I were just enjoying the shade as far south as it *extends*. This grove is not a vast forest. There's an open, freshly spaded milpa less than fifty meters off the road.''

''Oh boy! Okay. Just get the fat girl dressed and ready to run. Leave Pilar and these mules with me for now.''

''Très bien, if I can trust you not to shove a banana up either mule's derriere. What was that strange business all about, by the way?''

''It was her idea. She seems to be sort of warm-natured. Get going, dammit!''

Gaston chuckled and left. A few moments later Pilar got up, smoothed her skirts sedately, and came over to join him, asking if they were going to die. He said, "It's a little early in the morning for that, as well. Those rurales were in too much of a hurry to beat the bushes as they rode. So it wasn't a simple fishing expedition. They were on their way to some known address."

"Oh, God, do you think they know about our hideout back there?"

"Take it easy, querida. They won't find us there now. What is there for them to find if someone *did* turn you and Concepción in to the law? You didn't leave anything of value at the old house, did you?"

She shook her head and said, "No. Santa Maria and her candles are in my sleeping roll on Eduardo there."

"Your silver, too?"

She hesitated and said, "Sí, a little. You and Gaston are the main contraband, this trip."

"I'll bet. But that's your own business. My point is that there's nothing the rurales can use against us, even if that's where they're headed. Gaston and I kept our Anglo clothes and we certainly didn't leave any note for the milkman. I asked you before if there was a telegraph line out of that village, Pilar."

She nodded, giggled, and said, "Sí. If I had been able to answer at the moment I would have told you, then, there is one. It runs northeast along another road, to Mexico City. For why do you ask?"

He shrugged and said, "You're right. It was a dumb question. It's obvious someone wired the government about some damned body. It might or might not have been about us. Then Mexico City wired a rurale post closer to us to check something out. How come you never told me that road we took leads to a rurale post, Pilar?''

She shuddered and replied, ''I never knew it did, before. The road out of town is not the one we will be following all the way. It is only the easiest route to the hills. Once we start climbing, we take less-imposing old Indian trails, forking south off the main road running east and west, see?''

''I do now. Those rurales must be stationed on the far side of the Sierra Madres. They rode all night along the main line if they got this far by this morning. The only question left reads two ways. They could have ridden in such imposing numbers because crossing the Sierra makes them nervous, even via the main roads, or because they're after someone on this side of the passes that makes them nervous too.''

Pilar nodded soberly and said, ''Everyone who has ever heard of Captain Gringo has heard about him chopping up los rurales, more than once, with that machine gun!''

· He smiled thinly and said, ''Not this particular machine gun. But yeah, I'd stay the hell away from me and mine if I was a rurale, too.''

Gaston and Concepción joined them. Captain Gringo left the ammo belt in the Maxim's feed, but grunted it back aboard the mule and started lashing it in place on the pack saddle as he told Gaston, ''I think we're okay for now. But we'd better not stay here after all. It'll only take those bastards a few minutes to ride into town. If we're what they came to look for, it'll only be a few more minutes before they start back, trying to cut our trail. I don't know how *you* feel, but I don't want 'em doing that.''

Gaston nodded soberly and stared down at the ground, saying, ''Eh bien, neither we nor the mules have made any tracks in this adorable green turf. But we did leave a dusty road a few minutes ago, hein?''

Captain Gringo took the lead mule's halter line in hand and said, "Right. Follow me with the kicker. We're going to have to do something about that."

They led the mules back to the road. There, they told the girls to stay put as they led the two mules out to the center of the road, where the dust was a confusion of hoofprints going both ways. Then, walking backward, they backed the mules into the bananas again. Captain Gringo studied the road shoulder for a moment and said, "Okay, it reads that two mules went into the grove for some reason and four came out. How would you put that together, Gaston?"

Gaston shrugged and suggested, "Two mules coming out from town met two more under the bananas and they all went off somewhere together?"

"Yeah, neither we nor the girls left much in the way of human footprints in the sunbaked surface, and it gets even better when you consider there's no real difference between the shoes of a mule or a horse. If they think they're talking about four *riders,* it gets even harder to read. Let's cut across to that newly turned dirt and see if we can add some more artistic touches."

He led them all through the bananas to where, sure enough, he found himself facing a modest acre or so of freshly dug red dirt. The far side was enclosed by uncultivated lowland second growth. Mostly weed trees, with stubby young palmetto dominating. He looked east and west as he took a coil of rope from their pack saddle. Both ends of the milpa were hedged in as well with tangled spinach. He thought, then told Gaston, "Take the girls east along the tree line and work south into that palmetto and sea grape. I'd dig in at the southeast corner if I were you."

"Gladly. But what are you planning to do, mon général?"

"Hopefully, I'm going to account for the riders those first two riders met in this banana grove. Get going, dammit."

Gaston said, "Come avec moi, mes chéries. Dick wants to play by himself this morning."

As Gaston led the two girls away, Captain Gringo tied the lead of the biter to the tail of the kicker. Then he tied the end of the long rope to the tail of Roberto. He let the rope uncoil as it dragged while he held the kicker's halter and led them normally down the tree line to the west a ways. Then he let them go, picked up the slack rope near them, and let it run through his hands as he worked around the northwest corner of the milpa, walking backward to make sure he was leaving no heel marks in the grassy edge. He got to the far corner and moved east along the far side of the field the same way. The mules across the way were eating grass now as he dragged the long rope sideways across the bare clods, raising some dust but not leaving any sign anyone could read as anything more than breeze across the dusty soil. When he decided he'd positioned himself about right, he proceeded to haul the rope in hand over hand.

The mules didn't like it much. They both struggled and bounced around a bit as they were forced to cross the open milpa backward. The kicker tried to kick the biter's face off and was rewarded for his efforts with a good bite on the rump. So by the time Captain Gringo had them reeled in under the trees on the other side, they'd both steadied down, although they both rolled their eyes at him as if they thought he was loco en la cabeza while he untied them and got them moving the right way along the far tree line toward Gaston and the girls.

When he joined them at the southeast corner of the open field of fire, Gaston said, "Eh bien, I always knew you had artistique tendencies, Dick. Even from here, one can see how two riders crossed from the south-southwest, breaking into a très happy lope as they saw their other mounted friends waiting for them among the bananas, hein?''

Pilar was too smart to ask dumb questions. But fat Concepción said, ''I do not understand. There was nobody riding across the milpa just now. Deek dragged two pack animals across it backwards, no?''

Captain Gringo didn't answer as he led the mules deeper into the tangle and unlimbered the machine gun again. So Gaston explained, ''Mais non, you are mistaken, ma petite. When one *leads* pack animals, one generally leads them *forward*, walking beside them. So obviously, since there are no human footprints, and since unled animals seldom walk so strangely, two mounted people rode across the field this morning. Do not burden your mind with further thought on the moment, chérie. I admire you for your body rather than your brains, hein?''

Captain Gringo rejoined them with a Winchester for Gaston and the Maxim and an extra ammo belt for himself. As he set up a hasty albeit well-camouflaged machine-gun nest, Pilar asked if she and Concepción should get their own saddle guns. He said, ''No. If we can't stop 'em with a Maxim and a Winchester, forget it. I don't want you girls pointing guns at anything until I see how well you shoot. We'll enjoy some target practice as well as some sex a little farther from town. Right now, just keep your fannies down and your pretty yaps shut.''

Pilar said, ''I am frightened, Deek!''

He said, ''Welcome to the club. Better yet, I just changed the plans. Gaston, take them both back into the bushes a ways. Screaming dames make me nervous when los rurales are in my neck of the woods!''

Gaston said, "True. But won't you need me and this rifle if your droll ruse fails to work?"

"I'll need you and a whole infantry platoon if this machine gun jams on me. But move the dames and mules out of earshot anyway. Do it now. If they're coming at all, it'll be fairly soon. We're only a few minutes out of town, dammit!"

Gaston rose, gathered the girls and other livestock, and led them away, leaving Captain Gringo alone and feeling mighty lonely. He looked at the sky, figured it had been at least three-quarters of an hour since the rurales had passed the first time, and checked the head spacing of his Maxim. It was set the same way he'd adjusted it. So that was that, and what else could he do to pass some time, goddammit?

It was hot and sticky, even in the shade, and something itchy was crawling up his leg now, under his pants. He didn't swat it. Old tropic hands never swatted anything crawling over them until they made sure it wasn't a scorpion or worse. It felt like an ant. He sure *hoped* it was an ant.

There was nothing he could do about it right now. To keep from getting stung, bitten, or just squishy, he'd have to slowly stand up and gently shake his pants leg. A man couldn't do that while manning a machine gun on his belly. So the hell with it.

The Ice Age came and went. Man discovered the wheel and was about to lay the foundations of Rome by the time the creepy-crawly had made it up to his crotch and was tickling hell out of his sweaty balls. He'd just about decided that los rurales were through scaring him for the day and that suddenly dropping his pants would surprise whatever was in there with him before it could seriously damage his genitals, when, without warning, a mounted rurale rode out into the milpa, wheeled his horse, and called out, "Hey, sergeant! There are more hoofprints over *here!*"

Captain Gringo forgot the whatever crawling around in his pants as a dozen more riders joined the first in his machine-gun sights. He felt his trigger finger itch worse than his balls and told it to behave itself. It wasn't a good idea to open fire on rurales when at least half the bastards were still under cover!

The NCO who'd responded to the first rider's announcement reined in and looked down at the mule prints. The riders were spread out enough so that he had to raise his voice to be heard by everyone, including the Yank training a Maxim on him, as he decided, "Bueno. I get the picture now. Two riders coming from town rode into the bananas to meet whoever *these* two were. Ah hah! See how they moved out of town through the brush over that way? Look, right there is where they spotted their friends ahead, reined in, then loped to meet them."

Another rurale, who'd ridden farther back along the mule tracks, called out, "Shall we backtrack them through the palmetto, sergeant?"

The NCO shook his sombreroed head and called back, "For why? We don't wish for to find out where they came from. We wish to know where the motherfuckers *went!*"

A rurale sitting his horse closer to Captain Gringo seemed to be looking right at him as he pointed east and said, "If they took the road east we can head them off by cutting through the second growth *that* way, sergeant!" -

But the NCO, bless him, shouted, "Don't be an asshole. Roads were made for to keep a rider from tearing the hide off his horse as well as his knees. That's saw palmetto and sea grape you're so anxious to ride through, muchacho. Besides, we don't know which way they went after meeting in the banana grove. So let us think before we dash madly after who knows what, eh? To begin with, there is nothing here to say these hoofprints were left by Captain Gringo and that little Legion deserter. Lots of people ride horses, they tell me, and they also told me the two soldiers of fortune and those whores left town leading *two mules,* not *four horses!''*

Another rurale nodded, but said, ''Just the same, sergeant, someone rode most secretively through here. Don't you think the captain would want us to check them out, too?''

''Madre de Dios, do we have time to search for every sneaky person in Mexico! We are after big game, muchachos! I do not read the sign here as anything but simply skullduggery. Obviously four riders wished for to meet in those bananas secretly. Their reasons could have been most banal.''

Another rider broke cover to call out, ''Hey, sergeant, over here. Rosario just found a sign under a banana. He said to tell you it looks like someone was fucking a woman who moved her big ass a lot. The guy scraped the sod bare with his toes, too.''

The NCO threw back his head and laughed. Then he said, ''What did I tell you, muchachos? I see it all, now. A couple of naughty boys met a couple of naughty girls out here for to play slap and tickle where neither the padre nor their families were liable to notice. By now they are all back in the village, trying to look innocent about the grass stains on their clothing, no?''

The other rurales thought it was pretty funny and even Captain Gringo had to grin as he pictured it their way, which was close enough, when one thought about it.

The NCO said, ''Bueno. Let us be on our way, then. We still have to catch up with that goddamned Captain Gringo, wherever he's gone.''

As they all started walking their mounts back toward the banana grove, one asked their NCO if he wanted to check out the Red Cross column they'd met a while back again. They were almost out of earshot now, but Captain Gringo was relieved to hear the loud-mouthed NCO observe, "It's a waste of time and we were told to stay away from those busybodies in any case. Our informants in town say Captain Gringo tried to join the Red Cross people and was turned down. We are looking for two men and two women, afoot and leading mules. So, dammit, let's go *find* them!"

Captain Gringo didn't move a muscle as the Mexican lawmen moved out of sight and the creepy-crawly inside his pants started moving down the other leg, God bless it. He deliberately waited a good five minutes. Then he made himself wait another five before he decided they'd really left. To keep his hands busy while he lay doggo, he checked the action of his Maxim again. You could never do that too often, and there were times when you couldn't. The head spacing, feed mechanism, and firing pin were just as sound as they'd been the last time he'd looked. He tried to think of anything he hadn't already checked that morning. He'd checked everything but the bore, which was silly, since he'd cleaned the gun more than once along the way and hadn't gotten to fire it once. But what the hell. He removed the belt, leaving it close at hand in the grass just in case, and ejected the round in the chamber. He put his thumb in to reflect some light down the barrel. There wasn't any.

He frowned and moved back into the palmetto, dragging the Maxim and both belts after him. Then he rose to his knees, stood the Maxim on its breech, and looked down the muzzle. Then he started to swear a lot.

He took out his pocketknife, cut a handy sea-grape whip, and peeled it before ramming it down the barrel. He had to ram pretty good before he'd driven the long plug of clay out the far side!

He inverted the open breech to spill the now busted-up hard

clay. Then he used his improvised ramrod to scrub the last of it out of the lands, or at least clean the barrel enough so he could fire without blowing his own head off!

He picked up the gun and its belts and went to find Gaston, the girls, and the mules. Gaston noted the grim look on his face and asked if he'd seen a ghost he knew personally, or just a strange one.

Captain Gringo said, "Both," as he lashed the gun to the pack saddle again and added, "The rurales had a hasty peek and fell for our ruse. Someone tipped them off that we're back in Mexico. Someone else stuffed the barrel of this Maxim full of adobe. It's a good thing I didn't find that out the hard way! I think we're in trouble, Gaston."

"Merde alors, you just noticed? I told you that before we left Costa Rica! But who could the species of rat be?"

"How do you like your rats, alphabetical or numerical? The Mexican government wants us for everything but spreading the common cold. I don't think the U.S. Navy knows we're here. We'd never have bluffed the SP more than once if they had orders to look for a guy answering my description. The rurales know we were turned down by the Red Cross. Let's go with that for now. Anyone who can read could have seen one of the reward posters out on us when and if they went to the local telegraph office to wire home that they'd made it this far. It wouldn't have cost them as much to wire Mexico City while they were at it."

"True. But how would a species of Red Cross rat have been able to sabotage our machine gun, Dick?"

"I'm still working on that. I'm sure I cleaned the barrel a couple of times aboard the boat. I came back to the house right after I met those Red Cross guys and gals. I *should* have noticed if anyone crept in in the wee small hours, but the gun was right by the back door and said door was supposed to be locked.''

Gaston looked sheepish and said, ''Speaking for myself, there were times during the night when I would not have noticed a herd of elephants down the hall.''

Captain Gringo looked at Pilar, who was grinning, as he said, ''Yeah, that works. Any knock-around guy worth his salt could open a simple latch like that with a knife, and damned near everyone down here packs a knife. Have you girls had trouble with burglars in the past, Pilar?''

She said, ''No, Deek. But this is rather frightening! What if the intruder had not stopped in the back room? What if he had come in on us while we were . . .''

''He didn't have the balls,'' Captain Gringo cut in with a shrug, adding, ''They sent a sneak, not a killer. Probably wired a local police informer who wasn't about to take us on himself. It was a pretty neat trick, now that I think about it. If he'd taken the mules, we'd never have left town, and even los rurales avoid breaking windows they don't have to. They sent someone to make sure we were with two known guides, had him mess up the gun to shave the odds in their favor without tipping us off, and then, meanwhile, rode to meet us on the trail. Having met nobody on said trail by now, los rurales must be a little confused, too.''

Gaston opened the breech of his Winchester and held the rifle to his eye like a telescope before he gasped and swore in French, Spanish, and Arabic. Captain Gringo nodded and said, ''Don't just cuss about it, pal. Cut yourself a stick and clean the fucking mud out of your own bore!''

As Gaston did so, Captain Gringo checked all the other guns, and, sure enough, the girl's saddle guns as well as the repeaters he'd picked up the night before at the market had all been gummed up with clay.

He showed Pilar and Concepción how to get the crud out as he checked the supplies. Nothing had been stolen, and since most of the food was in cans he didn't see how they could have been poisoned. He threw away a sack of flour, telling Pilar, when she bitched, how easy it was to piss most anything through thin cloth. She blanched and said, "I do not think we wish for to go any farther with the two of you, Deek! Concepción and me were hired as guides, not as moving targets!"

He shrugged and said, "Okay, doll box. It's not far from here to your village and it's sure been nice knowing you. You can take your silver with you. You can take your plaster Madonna, too. But the guns and mules stay with us."

"That is not just, Deek! Why would you wish for to rob poor women who have been so good to you, eh?"

"It's not robbery, Pilar, it's simply survival. You don't need trail supplies to make it back to the village. We do, to get to Guatemala."

He didn't press the matter either way as the two female guides went out of earshot to have a chat about it. He just went on cleaning guns. When there was time, he would break out the gun-cleaning kit and do it right. Meanwhile, it was more important that they just shoot, if need be.

As long as he was at it, he cleaned Pilar and Concepción's carbines, too. He'd finished and was lashing everything back in place when they rejoined him. Pilar said, "We have been thinking. If you try to get through to Guatemala without us, you will never make it, and we will never get the final payment from the insurance company, no?"

"I was hoping you'd see it that way, doll box. Old Gaston's a lousy lay."

Concepción giggled and murmured that he was wrong. Pilar laughed too and said, "Bueno. We'll go on with you for now. But only if we do not brush with any more rurales again, eh? It is said los rurales make a habit of raping women they catch."

He raised an eyebrow. Pilar looked down and said, "All right, *that* part might not be so bad. But after they gang-rape female prisoners, they shoot them. That is *one* thrill we are not looking forward to!"

Things started looking up, in every way, as they worked their way east the rest of the day through brush that the rurale NCO had been right about. The slope kept getting steeper and the girls kept bitching about having to wade through overgrown thorny spinach without the usual siesta when the sun stopped fooling around and really heated things up. Pilar protested that she and Concepción never headed into the Sierra Madres by this route, since there didn't seem to be any route, goddammit. Captain Gringo just kept them all moving as he explained soothingly, "I know you girls are used to moving at night, when the roads are safer. But it's not dark out now, and those rurales will be tearing up and down every goat path around here until they get tired of looking for us."

"Sí, Deek. But meanwhile the heat is killing us, and what if we get lost?"

"How can we get lost, querida? We're looking for a mountain range running north and south from Alaska to Patagonia and we're going from west to east, uphill."

"Sí, but we do not know every inch of the Sierra, Deek. We only know the trails of a very modest part of it. If we wind up in some box canyon none of us have ever seen before . . ."

"We'll be in a hell of a mess," he cut in, adding,

"Meanwhile, nobody's shooting at us and we have to be heading into *some* damned part of the Sierra Madres. So pick 'em up and lay 'em down, quérida."

"Can't we stop for at least a short siesta, Deek? It is after noon and oh so hot!"

"I thought you were afraid of getting lost? We're under shade most of the time, we don't want to hit the high country after dark, and I want you up on a ridge for some educated looks around when we hit the serious Sierra Madres and . . ."

"You are talking like an idioto!" she cut in, adding, "We shall never make it to the open scablands in one day, no matter how fast we walk. The coast is more than a day's march from the true spine of the Sierra Madres."

He frowned and asked, "No shit? Then what's this slope we're pushing up, doll box?"

"The coastal range, of course. We have many hills and dales for to cross before we shall be in the real mountains."

He walked on a few paces, shrugged, and said, "Okay. So what are we trying to prove? I like siestas too."

As he tethered the mule to a sapling, Gaston did the same with the other and joined them, along with Concepción. The fat girl didn't ask questions. She simply flopped to the ground with a groan of sheer relief. But Gaston asked why they'd stopped, so Captain Gringo explained, "We're not going to make it anywhere important today. So we'll fort up here until it cools off some. Then we'll forge on until dark and make camp for the night. Any complaints?"

"Mais non. This seems a most pleasant picnic ground, save for the insects." He looked up through a gap in the tree canopy to add, "I had better break out a machete and play Robinson Crusoe, though. It looks like rain."

Captain Gringo didn't think it did, but Gaston had been down here longer, so he didn't argue as they made camp. He

did argue, however, when Concepción proceeded to pile a
mess of sticks together for a fire. He shook his head and said,
"Don't do that, Concepción. It's hot enough in this clearing
already."

She looked confused and asked, "But how am I to boil
water for our coffee, Deek?"

He said, "You're not. It's broad daylight. So let's let los
rurales *guess* where we are. Let's not send them any smoke
signals."

Pilar yelled, "Concepción, you are such a big fat fool I
can't stand it! Do you wish for to get us all killed?"

"No, I only wish I could have some coffee."

Captain Gringo left Pilar to explain the facts of life in
enemy country as he found a tree that looked reasonably easy
to climb, and climbed it. The discussion about campfire
smoke had reminded him that they were not alone in these
shrubby hills. He was a big man and the tree was swaying as
if it had noticed this by the time he'd worked high enough to
see out across the tops of the less imposing growth all around.
He saw that Gaston was right about the rain clouds coming in
from the southwest. When the wind was from that quarter
along this coast, it was talking about a gully-washing storm.
To the east he could see the distant purple peaks of the Sierra
Madres. They didn't look too far away. But mountains were
like that.

Closer, about ten miles to the northeast, he spotted a lazy
plume of blue wood smoke. He nodded to himself. The road
was over that way and the Red Cross expedition had taken
that route. Their Mexican guides had probably insisted on
stopping for la siesta. By now, if their guides knew as much
about the local weather patterns as they should, the other
party would be putting up their tents as well.

He didn't see any other smoke plumes in any direction. Los

rurales were either enjoying their own siesta back in the coastal village or, if really serious about this business, traveling Apache-style, too.

He climbed back down to see that Gaston had already thrown together two lean-tos, facing away from each other, the dirty old thing.

Pilar was under the palmetto thatch open to face the tethered mules. She was sipping from an open can of preserved tomatoes as he saw Gaston and Concepción were already out of sight under the other lean-to. He smiled crookedly and moved out to the mules. Pilar called out to ask what he was doing and he called back, "Going to take the packs off and let 'em graze on long leads."

She got up to join him, saying, "Bueno. But you do not have to keep them tied, Deek. They never stray far from Concepción and me."

"Yeah? Well, you must know more about mules than an old army man like me, then. It's fixing to rain fire and salt with maybe some summer lightning thrown in. Surely you hobble them at night up in the high country, Pilar?"

She shook her head and said, "No. We do not have to. Eduardo and Roberto are in love with us, you see."

He frowned and stared thoughtfully at the kicker, who'd just let out a yard of dong to take a piss as Pilar patted his muzzle. Captain Gringo shook his head and said, "No. I couldn't have heard that right."

Pilar laughed like a dirty little kid and said, "Of course not. You know I'm not *that* loose between my thighs, querido."

He laughed and said, "I should hope so. I know that while mules are sterile they're not sissies, but there's just no way any woman could serve a dong like that. A burro, maybe, but . . ."

She giggled and said, "Silly, we just jerk them off. Didn't

you know that old trick for to make a mule your lasting friend?''

''Not in *this* man's army. We used to just *hit* 'em a lot. Are you serious, Pilar?''

''Sí, it is fun for us, too, in a way. Concepción and me sometimes get most hot, telling each other dirty stories as we make the mules come. Once, Concepción got so excited, she tried to really do it with Eduardo, but of course they could not.''

He grimaced and said, ''That's sure a shame. But it probably saved her life.''

''Sí, that is what I told her. But you know how people get when they are really hot and have nobody for to fuck, eh?''

''Yeah, but why worry, in a world full of bananas?''

She grinned lewdly and took his arm to say, ''I do not see any banana trees around here, querido. But let us get under the shelter and I am sure we shall find a satisfactory substitute, no?''

He laughed, told her to just start without him if she couldn't wait, and unsaddled the mules while she moved sensuously back to the lean-to. A warm gob of rain plopped down on his wrist as he secured them on long leads, just in case, anyway. He'd heard circus-animal trainers used masturbation to keep their critters calm and friendly. He chuckled as he considered the work involved in jerking off an elephant. He wondered what else two oversexed girls did alone on the trail in their travels. He wasn't sure he wanted to know. He had nothing better to do for the next few hours and he wasn't really jealous about that green banana, but, hell, a guy didn't want to shove his personal treasure into anything really *disgusting*, right?

When he rejoined Pilar under the thatch, she was still sipping from the tomato can, but stark naked as she reclined on the improvised floor mat of fern fronds. She looked cooler than he felt. So he stripped to join her, and, bless Gaston's thoughtfulness, the ferns under them smelled clean and fresher than she did. He didn't fault her for her gamy body odors as he took her in his arms again. He'd been sweating like a pig all day too. So it tended to even out.

She drained the can and tossed it away as she lay back on the ferns to welcome him home between her widespread thighs. It was too hot and there was far too much codfish in the air right now to consider anything but old-fashioned missionary stuff. But as he entered her once more he was sure glad she'd suggested it. He'd almost forgotten how tight she was, for such an obviously adventurous little mutt.

They were both sloppy with sweat by the time they'd climaxed again together for the first time. Naturally she wanted more and naturally he didn't have to have his arm twisted as she twisted skillfully under him. But he heaved a great sigh of relief, just the same, when the sky opened up to dump sheets of silvery tropic rain, cooling the air under the lean-to pleasantly.

Pilar laughed and said, "Oh, thank you, Santa Maria! Even with a handsome man, there are limits to how much sweat one desires to fuck with. Let me up, Deek. I wish for to run out and get clean again!"

That made two of them. So, hand in hand, they stepped out into the downpour and let the warm sweet rainwater run down their naked bodies as they smiled at each other.

Over the wet hair on Pilar's shoulder he saw that other great minds had been running in the same channels. Gaston and Concepción were running around bare-assed in the rain like a couple of kids, too. They looked pretty silly. Gaston had a pretty lean and muscular body for a man his size and age. Concepción looked more like a circus fat lady taking a shower. There sure was a lot of her. But the falling rain veiled them both a bit and the details were Gaston's problem in any case. Gaston spotted them and waved. Captain Gringo waved back but called out, "Keep your distance, old buddy," adding in English, "I like an orgy as well as the next guy, but not when the other guys bring stuff like *that* to the party!"

Gaston laughed and called back, "Do not knock it until you try it, my fastidious youth. But I can see you have something at least as nice, so I shall not insist."

Pilar turned too, and waved at Concepción, calling out, "Isn't this more fun than being alone on the trail, Concepción?" Then she took another look at Gaston and added, with a lewd laugh, "Madre de Dios, I thought he was *little!*"

It started raining even harder, hiding some of the other couple's charms and cooling Captain Gringo's own erection more than he really needed. He was about to suggest getting back under shelter when a lightning bolt hit a tree not far away, and the two mules tried to bolt. They couldn't, thanks to the way he'd tethered them, but they were fighting the leads like hooked bass now. He said, "I'd better take some slack out of the ropes. I thought you said they never ran away, Pilar."

She said, "Get Eduardo. I'll take care of Roberto." So he ran over and hauled the nearest mule in closer to the tree it was tied to, punching its muzzle when it tired to bite his bare ass.

He got the mule tethered right, glanced around to see how Pilar was making out, and blinked in surprise. The shapely little mestiza was on her knees beside the mule, playing with its long dong as she cooed lovingly to it. The mule's eyes were closed in pleasure as the pretty girl jerked its ugly prong with both hands.

He moved closer, observing, "Well, he sure does seem to like what you're doing, doll box."

She said, "Sí, and it's making *me* hot, too! Why do you not take care of me as I take care of this big thing, Deek?"

He said, "That's just plain silly, Pilar." But she moved into a new and rather interesting position, with her bare brown rump thrust teasingly up at him as she knelt on both knees and one hand, jerking off the mule with the other. So he laughed, dropped behind her, and shoved it into her dog-style while the mule brayed in what sounded like passion, pain, confusion, or all three. The whole weird scene seemed to drive Pilar crazy, too. She started making hee-haw noises back at him, the mule, or both, as she arched her spine to respond to his thrusts while she went on stroking the full length of the rain-slicked pecker of the mule.

The two humans climaxed almost together, with Captain Gringo's coming in her triggering the excited Pilar's orgasm. Any lust he might still have felt was rapidly cooled by the sight of the mule's awesome ejaculation. He said, "Glugh!" withdrew from her, and added, "Let's go back to the lean-to and finish right. This is getting a little too rich for my blood, doll box."

She said, "I'll be with you in a minute. I have to take care of the other mule. The poor thing loves me."

He grimaced, got to his feet, and walked naked through the clean rain, feeling sort of dirty. He ducked under the overhang, lit another smoke, and reclined on one elbow, bemused, to watch Pilar jerk off the second mule. It was hard to tell, from here, which of them was enjoying it more. The oversexed little mutt was playing with herself with her free hand while she drove the excited beast nuts with long teasing strokes with the other. Captain Gringo couldn't have gotten his own dong back up with a block and tackle right now. Like most healthy young men, he liked his sex a *little* dirty. But enough was enough.

The second mule hee-hawed and shot its wad. Pilar laughed, got up, and ran over to the lean-to through the rain, shouting, "Oh, I am so passionate this afternoon, Deek!"

He said he'd noticed that as she dropped to the ferns beside him and pleaded, "Make me come again, por favor!"

He shrugged, put his free hand in her lap, and proceeded to massage her slippery clit. She thrust her pelvis up at him and hissed, "No, not with your hand, querido! I have my own hands, if I wished for to come that way! I wish for to be filled with cock!"

Somehow, that seemed more reasonable now than it had a few minutes ago. So he rolled her over, lifted her to her hands and knees, and got back into her dog-style. She giggled and said, "Sí, that does feel beastly. Put it to me that way as deeply as you can."

So he did, enjoying his claro as he smoked and humped her at the same time. His casual strokes drove her wild and she did most of the work as they had sex that way. She lowered her face to the ferns, with her back arched to thrust her brown rump higher as she moaned, "That is muy fantastico, Deek. It could not feel any better. But I can't help wondering what it would feel like if a woman could do it this way with a mule's big thing in her! Do you think I could be a little crazy?"

He said, "Yeah. Don't ever try it. For one thing, it'd probably kill you. For another, while I might be broad-minded about sharing you with a banana, I'll be damned if I'll go sloppy seconds with a jackass!"

•   •   •   •

The rain stopped later that afternoon. So they all got dressed and moved on. Fat Concepción was walking a little funny, and the mules were easier to handle now. So Captain Gringo made a mental note to tell Gaston to take it easy with his newfound girl friend, at least during daytime trail breaks. Pilar was chipper as ever, and he felt, if not really rested by his siesta, okay. Or at least he did until they topped a rise, he climbed another tree, and looked back.

The smoke he'd spotted rising from the Red Cross camp wasn't there now. They'd obviously moved on after the rain, too. But another column of smoke was rising above the treetops due west, between him and the village they'd left that morning!

He climbed back down and asked Gaston, "Could you have left a lit cigar under your lean-to, Gaston?"

"Merde alors, *how?* Everything was soaking wet by the time we broke camp. I built my own shelter a bit too low for a man aboard a rather immense femme who bounces awesomely, and so after she'd shoved my poor skinny derriere through the roof a few times . . ."

"Never mind your sex life, dammit. I know I tossed my own butts out into the rain and we built no campfires back there."

"Oui. So what are we talking about, Dick?"

"Smoke signals, I think. Can't say if it's rising from our siesta camp or just near enough to matter. But someone's sending up a hell of a lot of smoke back there. Green wood, too, like the Apache use when they want to signal pals a long way off!"

"Merde alors! Do you think we are being followed?"

"Think, hell, isn't it *obvious?*"

"Oui, our secret admirer who played sneaky sneaky with

our guns has to be tailing us for los rurales, unless the smoke
you spotted *is* los rurales!''

Captain Gringo shook his head and waved Pilar over to join
them as he told Gaston, ''If it was more than one or two
scouts they'd have moved in while we were playing bare-ass
slap and tickle in the rain back there. The real thing would
hardly want to give their position away with a campfire.
That's why I wouldn't let Concepción make coffee.''

Pilar asked him what was up. He said, ''We're being
tailed. One, maybe two people. Have you girls been getting
along with your neighbors in the village lately?''

She shrugged and said, ''If we had any real enemies back
there, they would have simply turned us over to the law by
now, no?''

He thought, nodded, and said, ''Los rurales don't get over
this way much, and when they do, they're not after little fish,
no offense. Some village two-face is after the rewards on
Gaston and me. They contacted los rurales to intercept us and
we got lucky. But to cover all bets, the informer or informers
were keeping an eye on us and we didn't throw *them* off our
trail. The pricks are dogging us, trying to signal los rurales.
So here's where you and Concepción get to show how good
you are.''

''What do you mean, Deek?''

''Hell, isn't it obvious, doll box? We have to either ambush
the sons of bitches or throw them off our trail. You girls know
this country better than we do. So which works best?''

Pilar looked confused and said she didn't know. He snorted
in disgust and said, ''Dammit, Pilar. You're supposed to be a
guide, not a don't-know!''

The mestiza looked like she was about to cry. Gaston said,
in a gentler tone, ''What my overexcited young companion is
trying to say is that it is up to you to show us either to some

jolly rise where we'll have an open field of fire down our back trail or, better yet, lead us through some species of terrain where we might find it easier to lose them." He turned to Captain Gringo and asked, "How far behind us are they at the moment, Dick?"

"Who knows? The smoke signal's a good four or five miles back. But there's nothing saying they had to *stay* there once they'd lit it!"

"Oui, and one can only see a few dozen yards through the shrubbery all about. I doubt they would be dogging us too closely. Regard how that disgusting species of mule left a clear hoofprint there and a steaming bowel movement over there, hein?"

Captain Gringo nodded and said, "Right. We have to get to a mile or so of bedrock or rough gravel at least. That's your department, Pilar. There ought to be some places · in these hills where the bones show through better. So where do we go from here?"

She said, "I do not know, Deek. I told you before, this is not the route Concepción and I usually take to the Sierra Madres!"

The tall American muttered, "Oh, shit. Okay. Let's just cut south for openers. We're on a ridge. So there ought to be some rimrock some damned where along it."

There was. But it wasn't close. It was almost sundown when the lead mule's steel-shod hoof struck sparks on a slab of old lava and, better yet, pissed and moaned when Captain Gringo led it onto solid rock beyond.

He slowed down, allowing the mules to pick their way gingerly across the smooth black shiny rock as it rose steeper. Gaston, leading the mule behind, was an even older hand at covering his tracks. So he didn't ask what they were doing, and when his own mule dropped a turd, Gaston stopped, picked it up, and threw it into the nearest cactus patch.

There was more cactus on all sides now as the ridge got too barren to support anything but dry country shallow-rooted vegetation. When Captain Gringo paused on a rise of the roller-coaster ridge, Gaston handed the lead to Concepción, joined the taller American, and observed, "If anyone is at all curious, within miles, they can *see* us up here, Dick."

Captain Gringo said, "I want 'em to. I don't know how far this rocky stretch runs south. Moonrise should be about eight tonight, right?"

"Oui. So what?"

"The sun'll be down in less than an hour. That gives us a couple of hours of total darkness. Come on. That next rise is even higher and dominates this stretch of open ground. We have to set up, up there, in broad daylight."

Gaston shrugged and went back to Concepción and the rear mule as Captain Gringo and Pilar led the way across the shallow saddle and up to the crest of the highest rise within miles. He told Pilar to hold the mule as he unlashed the machine gun and positioned it on a basalt outcrop to cover their back trail. Gaston led Concepción and the other mule beyond his improvised machine-gun position, tethered the mule, and walked back to Captain Gringo, saying, "Eh bien. Obviously anyone stupid enough to come along the ridge after us will be walking straight into a machine-gun muzzle. Mais just as obviously, anyone watching us from a discreet distance at the moment can *see* this if he has the brains of a gnat, non?"

"I sure hope so, Gaston. But just in case they're too shy to move in for a closer look, you'd better tell Concepción to make us some coffee. We can use it. We might not get much sleep tonight."

"You know, of course, that the smoke of even a discreet fire will be seen for miles if we build it atop this ridge?"

"That's what I just said."

Gaston shrugged and went to help Concepción gather fuel among the rocks. So in a little while they had a modest fire of dry yucca stalks and smokier cactus roots. By the time the coffee and beans were ready, Captain Gringo had forted his machine-gun position with an imposing wall of rocks and the sun was about to wink out on the western horizon.

He joined the others around the little fire, hunkered down, and said, "Okay, boys and girls. Eat your beans and wash 'em down, pronto. We'll be moving out in a few minutes."

Gaston nodded. But the girls looked confused. So Captain Gringo explained, "We're not making camp here. We want them to *think* we're making camp here, see?"

Pilar asked, "But, Deek, where are we to camp tonight?"

He said, "Beats the shit out of me. If the moon stays up and the country's open enough, we may wind up a hell of a ways from here before morning. Eat your beans."

They did, and, as each finished, Captain Gringo took their cans and peeled the paper off the shiny tin. Then, in the purple light just after sundown, he placed the cans artistically around his machine-gun nest to catch the next dawn light. Pilar asked him what the people following them were supposed to think the cans were, and he said, "Let *them* worry about it, doll box. Would you rush madly up a slope at anything going glitter glitter by the dawn's early light?"

Concepción said she was tired. Gaston made her get up anyway, and as they joined Captain Gringo and Pilar, he said, "Eh bien, I like it! Now, since it is dark enough, we backtrack, non?"

Captain Gringo shook his head and said, "Why bother? Pilar says she doesn't know where the hell we are anyway."

He picked up the Maxim, carried it to his mule, and lashed it back in place under its tarp as he explained, "We're bound to leave signs going down the slope to the east. Doing so closer to them would just make it easier to cut our trail. How would *you* move in on this position if you were them, Gaston?"

"I wouldn't. I'd dig in at the tree line and wait for my rurale friends to catch up with my smoke signals. They don't pay police informers enough to rush uphill at machine guns, hein?"

"Not unless they're nuts. Okay. It's too dark now for anyone any distance away to see what we're doing. But it's still light enough to get down the slope to the east without busting our necks. So what the fuck are we waiting for?"

Crossing the woody valley to the east in the dark was a bitch. They'd never have made it up the far slope had the moon not risen in time to give them a little light on the subject. After that the going got easier. They found themselves atop a flat mesa, paved with rimrock and open, save for an occasional clump of cactus or yucca. So they made good time, for a change, and moonset found them threading their way up a sandy dry wash. Concepción and both mules were starting to balk at going on, and not even Captain Gringo fancied tripping over chaparral in the dark, so he called a halt.

Pilar flopped to the sand and told Concepción to build a fire. Captain Gringo said, "We'll do no such thing. We won't camp in this wash, either. I don't like to wake up under a flash flood. We'll bed down up above, in the brush. If we throw tarps over the branches we won't have to leave lean-to evidence in our wake and we'll still be dry enough if it rains again.''

Nobody bitched about it much but the mules, who were tough to get up the steep bank. They tethered them farther into the chaparral, unsaddled them, and, since they couldn't graze in such dry brush, watered them and put nose bags with some parched corn on them. Captain Gringo told the girls not to jerk them off and set up his own bedroll under a tarp near the rim of the wash, with his machine gun handy.

The night was clear and the tropic stars were bright, but it was still dark as hell, now that the moon was down. So he assumed the lady joining him right after he'd undressed and stretched out naked atop the bedroll was Pilar, until he started to take her in his arms and found his arms were full indeed. He frowned and asked, ''Concepción?''

It was a dumb question. Nobody else within miles could have been shoving such huge bare tits against his naked chest. But he had to say *something*.

She snuggled closer, which was a little awesome when that much naked flesh was involved, and said, ''Sí. Gaston said to tell you he and I had made a ghastly mistake. I do not know what that means, but I think you are pretty.''

''You're pretty, too,'' he lied gallantly. ''But I'm not sure there's room on this roll for you, me, and Pilar.''

The fat girl giggled and said, ''Silly. Pilar is with Gaston tonight. You see, when I told her of his odd habits in bed . . .''

He laughed and said, ''Yeah, she would want to try sixty-nine with a novel partner. But what was that about you and Gaston making some kind of mistake?''

''He is crazy. Do you know where he wishes for to put his thing all the time?''

''I sure wish you wouldn't tell me. I'm having enough

trouble adjusting to this weird situation. Suffice it to say you're an old-fashioned girl, right?''

"Sí. I do not mind a *little* silly business with an hombre, if he treats me right once I am inflamed. But Gaston and I do not seem to have been made for each other.''

He was too polite to observe that she didn't feel like she was made for *anyone*, save perhaps an elephant seal. She had to weigh two fifty or more, and she was short. He had to admit her smooth skin felt sort of nice against his as she moved ponderously to press more of it against him. But when she slid one huge thigh over his waist it felt like a side of beef.

Even knowing that her movement had positioned her love box, wide open, inches from his own confused virility wasn't doing as much for him as she no doubt expected it to. She hugged him closer with an arm as big around as either of his legs and asked shyly, "Aren't you going to kiss me, querido?''

That seemed fair. Her face, at least, hadn't been too awful the last time he'd looked. She wouldn't have been half-bad, in fact, had she been maybe a hundred or so pounds lighter. But he had to think about this situation. Damn that goofy insurance company. Couldn't they have hired a couple of better-looking girl guides, if they had to be nymphomaniacs?

She sobbed, "I knew it. That damned Pilar always gets the good-looking ones. Everybody thinks I am too fat!''

"Well, fair is fair, Concepción. Maybe if you cut down on starchy foods . . .''

She started to cry. He said, "Oh, for God's sake," took a deep breath, and kissed her. It wasn't as awful as he'd expected. She kissed back sort of sweetly. More like a little girl than a sea elephant in fact. But from the way she tongued him and ran her hand down between them to grab his confused manhood, he knew she was no blushing virgin.

She whimpered as if in pain when she felt, still kissing him, how soft he still was. He kissed her harder to cheer her up, put a hand to one of her huge breasts, and, what do you know, he wasn't quite as soft anymore. But it still felt weird as hell to fondle and kiss so much female all at once. He felt revolted and attracted at the same time. He knew she'd be hurt as hell if he stopped now. So, since he needed her services as a guide a hell of a lot more than he desired her as a woman, he gallantly rose to the occasion and threw caution to the winds. But even after he'd made up his mind to give her the old college try, it was sort of complicated.

He rolled Concepción on her broad back and got on top of her. He sure as hell didn't want to be *under* her. He had it up enough to serve an average woman now. But Concepción wasn't an average woman. She was fat as hell. Her big belly felt like an extra, misplaced breast, a big one, against his own, and though she'd spread her huge thighs as far as they'd go, his hips were still cushioned in a soft smooth cradle a hell of a ways off the ground. Her huge rump, however, presented her pelvis at an angle most women would have needed two pillows or more under their hips to manage. So it tended to even out, and with some effort he was able to get the head in position to enter her. When he did, she sobbed, "Oh, glorioso!" and bear-hugged him tightly to her big soft torso as she dug her heels in and thrust her considerable hips up to meet him. He was pleasantly surprised, too, to find such a nice love box throbbing along the full length of his now fully aroused shaft. So the rest was easy and not bad at all, if a man enjoyed playing bouncy bouncy on a feather bed with a very pleasant hole in the mattress.

She crooned, "Oh, you are so big, Deek!" and didn't get it when he laughed like hell. She giggled and said, "Sí, I know we are both being wicked and we shall no doubt land in hell someday. But tonight I am in heaven and, quién sabe, the padres *could* be wrong, no?''

He kissed her to shut her up. She was fat and stupid, but not a bad kid, once you got to know her. So he concentrated on knowing her, in the biblical sense, and since she'd started out a lot more eager to get laid than he had, she came first.

It felt sort of like screwing an earthquake. Her big body heaved and trembled under him in wave after wave of passion as he just hung on for dear life, afraid to fall from such a height, while she moved it inside her with no effort on his part at all, until near the end, when he pounded her hard and ejaculated in her deeply. They both went limp in each other's arms and Concepción sighed and said, "Oh, that was so lovely, Deek. I thank you from the bottom of my heart. That was just the way I wished for to be loved."

Love was a pretty strong term for the way he felt about the fat mestiza, but she was a nice change from the prettier but dirtier—in every way—Pilar. So he kissed her again, as a pal.

She sobbed. "Oh, Deek! You do not find me loathsome, now that you have had your way with me?"

He chuckled and said, "As a matter of fact, I think you're kind of pretty." What else was a guy supposed to say on top of a lady?

Concepción must have been used to rougher gentlemen. She gasped and asked, "Es verdad? You do not use me as a fat cow when you can get nothing better?"

"Don't talk dumb, Concepción. I've never laid a cow in my life."

She giggled and said, "Your thing is twitching inside me, Deek. For why is it doing that? Are you making it do that?"

"No, I guess it has a mind of its own. You're twitching pretty good too. We'd better do something about that."

As he started moving again she gasped and said, "I can't believe it! You wish more, without even changing positions?"

He just kept laying her without comment. He couldn't think of any other position that would work with a dame this size, and the one they were in was already unusual as hell. He supposed it could be said that they were doing it old-fashioned. But it was still quite a novelty to be on his knees, almost dog-style, with the dame face up on the bottom. She was much shorter than he was, standing up, but there was so much of her to cover, lying down, that he felt like a little boy making it with a grown woman and had to crane his neck to kiss her. He settled for kissing her under the chins, all three of them, as he started moving seriously again.

She climaxed twice, awesomely, before he did again. So he felt it wouldn't be considered impolite if he rolled off after doing his duty to her. He'd been pleasantly surprised at how nice it had been, but while he was usually up to more than twice with a really attractive partner, there was no sense being silly about old Concepción.

He lay flat on his back, glad to be once more on terra firma, as Concepción sat up to stare down adoringly at him in the starlight. It was cooler and drier at this higher altitude. But not cool enough to get under the blankets. He smiled back, wondering if he wanted to smoke first or just go to sleep. Concepción said, "Oh, you make me feel so passionate, Deek."

He said, "That's nice. You make me feel passionate, too."

He didn't mean it. He was naturally still semierect after being treated so nicely. But he'd had a hard day and two women, so what the hell. Concepción said, "Bueno," and proceeded to get on top.

He gasped and said, "Hold it! I'm not sure we're going about this right, querida!" But she'd already forked a huge thigh over him and was lowering her awesome mass on him. So he braced himself for a steamroller attack as she reached down, grabbed him by the root, and lowered herself onto it.

She said, "Oh, it goes even farther up inside me this way, no?"

That was for damned sure. With her own weight on her thighs, they spread farther and, to his pleasant surprise, held most of her weight as she arched her spine, threw back her head, and rested some more of it on her locked elbows with her hands on the ground behind her. She didn't look nearly as fat in that position. The arch of her torso pulled her soft belly up and flattened it some as she thrust her big nipples up at the Milky Way and tried to scrape stars from the sky with them as she bounced up and down the full length of his shaft.

He reached down and started working on her clit with his thumb to help her, and it helped her a lot, since she was already hot as a two-dollar pistol. She contracted almost painfully on him in orgasm and fell off backward, just as he was starting to get interested. So he rolled to his hands and knees to finish in her right, making her come yet again and, this time, with him.

That did it. So as they lay together, sharing a smoke before going to sleep, Concepción said she had never been so happy before. But Captain Gringo was beginning to feel like a shit. Fun was fun, but he doubted that he could sustain a romance like *this* very long.

The next morning they worked upslope through the chaparral to a much higher ridge. Beyond, to the east, loomed the jagged sawteeth of the Sierra Madres. Behind them, to the west, rose a column of white smoke. Gaston said, "Merde alors! They didn't fall for our ruse, Dick!"

Captain Gringo said, "Tell me something I didn't know. They're using green wood in that soggy valley we cut across in the dark after dropping down off the rimrock. So tell me how they trailed us in total darkness?"

Gaston shrugged and suggested, "Perhaps they assumed it was a ruse because you were so obviously bent on setting up an ambush in plain view. If they were closer in than we assumed, they might have simply moved in as we were moving out, heard us crashing through the brush below us, and . . ."

"That still makes them damned good, as well as mighty determined," Captain Gringo cut in, scanning the rest of the skyline as he added, "If los rurales are following smoke signals, they're not sending any of their own."

"But of course not, Dick. They only have to ride in the direction of the smoke their triple-titted scout or scouts keep sending skyward. But look at the bright side. If los rurales had caught up, there would *be* no smoke, hein?"

The girls of course had been listening, and since Pilar was the smarter as well as the dirtier of the two, she asked, "Is it not possible that what we see is the Red Cross people having breakfast, Deek?"

He shook his head and said, "Not unless their own guides like to go out of the way. They were following the regular trail to our north, last time we spotted *their* smoke. We've been working our way up here for quite a while. So by now the Red Cross expedition should have been moving pretty good for a while, too. They sure as hell wouldn't have cut in *back* of us across our trail. Thanks to the easier going on the road, they should be, hell, way over *that* way. We'd better do some moving too, if we expect to catch up with 'em."

He started to lead them down the eastern slope of the ridge. Gaston handed the lead of his own mule to Concepción and fell in beside the other soldier of fortune as he asked, "Just how much catching up do we intend, my long-legged youth? I thought the idea was to tag along behind them at a très discreet distance, non?"

"It still is. I want them to catch any heat ahead."

"Oui, but there seems to be more heat *behind* us at the moment, if I am any judge of smoke. Once we cut over to the main trail, won't that make us easier for our followers to track?"

"Hell, Gaston, they've been tracking us just fine ever since we left the village! So let's at least have those Red Cross greenhorns between us and anyone coming the other way. I don't intend to follow in their footsteps blindly, of course. As it gets more open and easier to see from ridge to ridge, we'll shadow the Red Cross expedition bandito-style, see?"

"That part makes sense. Meanwhile, what are we to do about the people shadowing *us* bandito-style?"

"I don't know yet. First we have to figure out how in the hell they're *doing* it! We might make it a little tougher for them if our trail cut across another party's now and again, right?"

"Oui, that makes sense. A mule track is a mule track and the Red Cross people are leading a droll number of mules. If we dropped onto the road behind them, followed it as far as some hard pan or solid rock, and simply faded into the bushes for a peep-peep . . ."

"That's what I just said. Go back and make sure we don't lose that other mule. Ah, you and Concepción are still on good terms, right?"

Gaston chuckled and said, "We are old friends, even if she does not enjoy French loving as much as Pilar. Why do you ask? Do you want the skinny one back already?"

"You and the mules can have her. Just wanted to clarify the current sleeping arrangements. Let's move it out."

They did. The next slope was even steeper and the cover was lousy. So when Concepción begged him to stop halfway up so they could rest, Captain Gringo shook his head and said, "I told you to get some sleep last night, querida. We're pretty little moving dots to anyone who's watching from that ridge behind us, and somebody probably is. We'll take a break in that saddle up ahead. I want to see if any pretty little dots are dumb enough to follow us up this open slope in broad-ass daylight!"

By the time they reached the saddle, even Captain Gringo's legs were feeling it. So they pushed into the denser chaparral along the ridge and flopped down wearily. Captain Gringo was covering their back trail. So it was Gaston who spotted what was in the valley beyond and crawled back to tell him about it.

Gaston said, "The Red Cross expedition has left the road over the Sierra to follow an adorable streambed south, over in the next valley."

Captain Gringo whistled Pilar over, told her to watch and give a holler if she spotted anything moving up the bare slope at them from the west, and moved across the saddle with Gaston for a look-see.

The valley to their west was wide and flat-bottomed with a winding mountain stream running north against the Red Cross expedition's line of march to the south. They made an imposing sight, strung out like that. The ten nursing sisters were mounted sidesaddle aboard as many Spanish mules. The khaki-uniformed men were on foot, leading the others, loaded with supplies. Two white-clad Mexicans led at the head of the long column, each leading a more modestly laden burro. They looked like they knew where they were going. A narrow path ran alongside the stream, cutting across most of the oxbows through the wild mustard and cactus clumps down there. Captain Gringo turned to wave Concepción over to them. When she joined them, he said, "There they are. So where are they going?"

Concepción frowned thoughtfully and said, "En verdad, I do not know, Deek. I know that rio. We have often watered there. But that is not the way for to get to Guatemala."

He asked, "Are you sure?"

She said, "Sí. At the south end of the valley the rio comes out of a box canyon. That path they are on is merely a deer trail. It leads nowhere important. They must be most estupido, no?"

Captain Gringo said, "Son of a bitch!" and ran for the tethered mules, yelling at Gaston to stay with the other and the girls as he started to lead the mule with the machine gun riding on it along the ridge to the south.

Gaston did no such thing. He caught up, panting, and asked, "Where are we going in such a hurry? I agree our European and Yankee friends have been sold out. But what is that to us? They said they did not need our services, remember?"

"They were wrong. I told you to guard the girls, dammit."

"Against what? The ambush is most obviously the way you are going. Nobody is seriously after the girls, and Concepción for one is not about to run away. You should be ashamed of yourself, Dick. I told her to tell you she was a delicate child."

"Shut up and drag this fucking mule if you want to help. I'll take the point."

He handed the lead to Gaston and moved up the next rise in a running crouch, dropping to his knees behind some brush for another look-see. Nothing. He ran down into the next saddle and up the next rise. He was even with the head of the column to his left now. That wasn't good enough. So when he didn't spot anything from that rise either, he moved on.

They'd outdistanced the slower-moving column by a quarter of a mile when Captain Gringo spotted what he was looking for, turned on one knee, and called back to Gaston, "Leave the mule there. But break out the Maxim and get it up here on the double!"

There were a good two dozen men down the slope below him to the east. But they were not the rurales he'd seen before. Rurales didn't dress like Mexican bandits, even though they acted just as nasty at times.

The guys lying in wait for the Red Cross expedition had chosen pretty good cover behind rocks and bushes, as far as anyone looking up from the valley floor went. They were wide open to Captain Gringo, with their backs to him. So that part wasn't the problem. The problem was that the damned Red Cross column was coming around the bend right now and a jerk-off in a big black sombrero was getting to his feet, waving it. The egg was about to hit the fan, and where was his damned machine gun?

He turned to curse Gaston as the Frenchman staggered up the slope to him with the Maxim on one shoulder and an ammo box in his free hand.

Captain Gringo grabbed it, armed it, and turned to move down the slope with it just as the bandits opened fire on the Red Cross column!

The treacherous guides, of course, had lit out cross-country to get out of the line of fire the moment they spotted the signal. So the first thing the bandits hit was the poor khaki-clad sucker leading the first supply mule. Another Red Cross worker folded like a jackknife to hit the dust beside him, while the rest of the column scattered in every direction, abandoning their supply mules just as they were supposed to.

It was a swell little ambush, until Captain Gringo opened up with the machine gun as he charged down the slope behind them.

It wasn't scientific. The book said the new weapon was supposed to be mounted on a tripod and adjusted for elevation and traverse with cute little knobs. But for a guy firing a machine gun from the hip, Captain Gringo did a pretty good job on the bandits. He swept from right to left, sending big hats and little gobs of bloody flesh flying, then dug in his left heel and traversed right at lower elevation to make sure of any possible survivors. He managed two full sweeps and a half before the belt ran dry. Gaston ran down to him with another and he put it in. There was only one slob trying to rise from the dust and busted-up chaparral now. So Gaston said, "Allow me," and blew the side of the bandit's head off with his .38.

Captain Gringo nodded in satisfaction and moved down through the grim results of his machine-gun fire, saying, "Reload and cover me. They might not know we're on their side."

"Merde alors, what difference does it make, since they were stupid enough to come out here without guns of their own?"

"They've got guns now. If they've seen the light yet. We just bought 'em two dozen here, to go with the Spencers I picked up for the dumb bastards."

By the time they'd crossed the valley floor, the shaken survivors were starting to make sense out of all the noise, and a couple of Red Cross men were coming to meet them. One called out in very bad Spanish and Captain Gringo replied, "We'd do better in English or French, pal. I don't see your guides anywhere. So they're probably on their way to rat on you to some *other* bandits they know! In case you haven't figured it out yet, this primrose path they led you down doesn't *go* anywhere. Where's Dr. Fitzke?''

One of them turned to point at two women kneeling over a still figure on the ground near the stream as he said, ''He's dead. The bastards *killed* him, and we came here to *help* these people!''

''Welcome to Mexico. If you still want to go to Guatemala, this ain't the way to get there. I'm Dick Walker. This is Gaston Verrier. We *do* know the way to Guatemala. If you want to get there our way. Who's in charge now, with Doc Fitzke dead?''

They looked at each other blankly. Captain Gringo said, ''That's what I thought. Oh, well, you're a new outfit. We can probably whip you into shape before you all manage to get yourselves killed.''

He could see soon enough that it wasn't going to be easy. He sent Gaston to bring the girls and their mules down from the ridge as the scattered survivors of the Red Cross expedition either chased other mules or gathered around him like lost sheep, which they were, in a way.

One stupid American girl in the party must have been reading the papers a lot, since she was the one who said, ''There's a notorious American renegade and soldier of fortune named Richard Walker. They call him Captain Gringo. I surely hope you're not another Dick Walker!''

He shrugged and said, ''What can I tell you, it was a bum rap? I didn't just smoke up those bandits for you to win a popularity contest. If you don't like my company, find someone else to lead you through the Sierra Madres. You kiddies must have noticed by now that the rules of polite society ain't as polite down here.''

Another girl, who looked like the little brunette he'd saved in the marketplace the other night, said, "We're Red Cross workers, not a judge and jury. I vote we settle the matter here and now with a show of hands. All in favor of following this gentleman and his friends, raise their right hands like so!"

Most of them did. But a red-faced guy with a clipped British accent said, "Not so fast, you lot. We don't know a thing about this man, and Gloria says he's an outlaw! How do we know he's telling us the truth? How do we know he won't lead us into something sticky?"

Before Captain Gringo could hit him, the little brunette stamped her foot and said, "Oh, don't be such an ass, Cecil! The guides poor Dr. Fitzke hired just led us into something sticky, and Dick here was kind enough to get us out of it with that nice machine gun! He saved Trixie and me from another sticky wicket in the marketplace the other night as well, now that I've had a closer look at him."

Another British male accent, to the credit of the empire, said, "Here here, Pam's right, you know. Wouldn't make sense to shoot bandits if one *was* a bandit, what?"

Cecil muttered, "Not unless he was with another gang. But I see I'm outvoted. So I suppose we'll just have to see who's right, in the end."

The other Britisher said, "I'm Lauder, ah, captain. Since you seem to know the form here, what do you suggest we do next?"

Captain Gringo glanced at the sun and said, "There's plenty of daylight left. You can begin by breaking out some shovels and burying your own dead. Don't bother with the bandits. Dat's why buzzards was born. But we'd better send a detail upslope to gather their guns and ammo."

"I say, the Red Cross doesn't carry weapons, captain."

''That's what those bandits just noticed. Any *other* outlaws in these hills have you down as sissies too. But two dozen rifles and at least that many pistols ought to make it tougher for the next bunch we run into. I've got some Spencer repeaters for you, too, if my pal ever gets here with 'em.''

The one named Cecil shook his head and said, ''Impossible. The charter is quite clear on the matter. We are simply not allowed to wear these armbands and carry guns at the same time!''

Captain Gringo swore under his breath, then said, ''So take the armbands off and *arm* yourselves, dammit! Do you think anyone up in these hills gives two hoots and a holler about international law? Man, they don't pay any attention to *Mexican* law, and as far as Mexico City cares, you guys and gals are completely on your own up here. There's nobody looking out for this outfit but thee and me, and if thee doesn't start to make some sense, I'm going on without you! There is no way in hell my pals and me can cover a column this size with our own few gun hands. So what's it gonna be?

They had to think about that. So he let them mutter among themselves as he spotted Gaston coming in alone with one mule and went to meet him.

Gaston wore a puzzled frown as he said, ''The girls must not have enjoyed our company as much as I assumed from the way Pilar blew me last night. They took off with the other mule and no doubt their silver.''

Captain Gringo nodded and said, ''They didn't have any silver.''

Gaston frowned and asked, ''Are you suggesting they were up to some sort of skullduggery, Dick?''

''Who else stuffed that adobe in our guns, the tooth fairy? The insurance company offered them a lousy four hundred bucks to get us across the border and back alive. We're worth over a thousand apiece to Mexico alone. So why go to all that work when you don't really have to?''

"Merde alors, you might have let me in on your suspicions before I ate both their pussies, Dick!''

Captain Gringo chuckled and said, "I didn't have anything to go on but suspicion till they verified it just now by tipping their mitts. But you've got to admit there were a lot of funny things going on around those funny dames.''

Gaston thought before he nodded and said, "Eh bien, I can add the figures, now that I observe the final equation. Either of them slipping out to mayhaps take the pee-pee could have stuffed our gun barrels within a few seconds, and I did find it odd that though they said they were carrying silver to smuggle, they never bothered to *check* it, after knowing we had been alone with their own pack saddle. The wild sex was of course to keep us contented and off guard, although one hopes they didn't fake *every* orgasm, hein?''

Captain Gringo said, "All but the banana bit back there in the grove when los rurales rode by. Pilar needed an excuse to be flat on the ground when she gave out such a good yell. Fortunately, they failed to hear her. They were anxious to meet us at her house, I guess.''

"Ah, oui, that was the only time she seemed so delicate. But may one assume they'll pick up their confederate who was trailing us so well on their way back to town?''

"What confederate? Nobody trails *me* that good, dammit! I was using tricks I learned in Apache country, the hard way.''

"But the smoke signals . . . Ah, how stupid of me.''

"Don't feel bad. I wasn't sure either, until just now. But, yeah, it would have been easy enough for either of 'em to leave a cigar butt burning with its unlit end under a hastily gathered pile of tinder and green wood from time to time.''

"Perfidity, thy name is Woman. May we assume it's safe to forget about los rurales for now?"

"For now, probably. They won't want to go anywhere near rurales on the trail, after failing. When they said they were nervous about rurales they were telling the truth, as well as showing common sense. Our oversexed police informers are still petty criminals and los rurales are bound to arrest *somebody* after riding all this way."

Gaston stared beyond him at the Red Cross column and said, "Oui, we are well south of the road, and in bandit country where possible victims of los rurales tend to shoot back. But that, unfortunately, is all I can tell you. I have no idea how to get to the border from here, do you?"

Captain Gringo shook his head and said, "No. But don't tell any of these greenhorns. I just told 'em we were fixing to lead them through the Sierra Madres."

"But how, Dick? Their guides betrayed them and our guides were trying to betray us. How on earth are we to lead them anywhere in these hills without one trustworthy guide?"

"I never said it was going to be easy. I just said we'd do it."

The Red Cross workers weren't all stupid. So a couple of dozen of the men and a couple of the girls decided it would be fair if they carried guns without their red crosses showing. One of the nursing sisters, of course, was little Pam, who turned out to be Canadian and said she'd hunted some with her dad's old Spencer and knew how to handle a .45 as well.

Captain Gringo left them to tidy up as he and Gaston borrowed a pair of riding mules to scout upstream, just in case Concepción had fibbed about that box canyon, too.

She hadn't. The water came over an imposing sheer cliff at the head of the valley in what would have been a pretty waterfall, if they'd been looking for such scenery. As Captain Gringo sat atop his mule, bareback, staring morosely up at the falling water, Gaston observed, "Eh bien, the trouble with lying women is that sometimes they tell the truth. At least now we know that they were the real guides the company hired and not a pair of ringers, hein?"

"Yeah. I said I figured they left the silver behind because they didn't intend to travel all the way with us. That bullshit about old Caballero Blanco was more razzle-dazzle. So watch out for white hats. He could be on either side of the border."

As he wheeled his mule around, Gaston drew his .38 without a word of warning and emptied it into a nearby clump of greasewood. Captain Gringo swore as his mule shied, steadied it, and asked, "Gaston, why in the hell did you do that?"

"You told me to watch out for white hats. I just spotted a white shirt in those bushes, I think."

"You *think*, you trigger-happy old goat?"

Gaston dismounted, reloading on the safe side of his mule as he replied. "Cover me if you persist in making such an obvious stationary target of yourself, hein?"

Captain Gringo dismounted, pronto, and drew his own revolver as the little Frenchman moved in, gun leveled. Gaston circled the clump, lowered the .38 to his side, and said, "Eh bien. I don't need reading glasses after all."

Captain Gringo joined him to see two white-clad bodies sprawled in the dust on the far side of the greasewood. He whistled and said, "Nice shooting, Gaston. I didn't see a fucking thing!"

"In truth, I only saw a patch of white. But as you say so

often, what the hell. We knew these runaway guides had to have run *somewhere*, non?''

''Yeah, and, dammit, neither of them had guns, thanks to the odd views of the late Herr Doktor Fitzke! They were only hiding from us, scared skinny, no doubt. I wish you'd given me a chance to have a chat with them first, Gaston.''

''Had I known they were both unarmed, I would have. But in these hills one does not meet many such people, Dick. Let us regard what they might have in their pockets, non?''

They each dropped by a different corpse to pat it down. Both false guides were packing a little pocket change, which could always come in handy. Captain Gringo pocketed his, saying, ''Nothing but Mexican money on this guy. Wait a second. He had something in his shirt pocket.''

Captain Gringo took the folded paper out and opened it as Gaston said, ''This one had a couple of Guatemalan coins as well. So, like the girls, they might have known the way, but just did not wish to show it to anyone. Like our *own* amusing guides, they saw an easier way to make the buck. What is that, Dick, a map?''

''Yeah. Unfortunately, not a good one. It's hand-drawn. Shows how to get this far and ends with a big fat question mark above that waterfall over there. This X marks the spot where the bandits were waiting. The sons of bitches really set old Fitzke up in advance.''

''We knew that already. None of the bandits we shot up just now could have been this species of Caballero Blanco. But if one band of outlaws knew that all these good things, and lovely ladies, were coming this way, who is to say what our gallant Guatemalan liberator knows, hein?''

''Do you always have to be so fucking cheerful? Hold it. There's a dotted line here. Or there was. Someone tried to erase the pencil marks with a lousy eraser.''

He held the map at a different angle to the light and said, "Yeah, it's some sort of trail, leading down into this valley from due east. Those bandits must have taken the next north-south valley down from the main post road through the Sierra, then cut over that ridge to the east and dug in on the west slope to wait for the column."

"How sneaky of them. But so what?"

"If they used another trail in another valley, they must be used to riding it. If we go over that ridge to the east, we'll wind up on the same trail."

"Or perhaps their hideout, Dick? Bandits down here move about like the armies, rebel or official, avec baggage and dependents. They never send their full force on a raid and . . ."

"Dammit, Gaston," Captain Gringo cut in, "I keep telling you I scouted Apache in my misspent youth. I know all too well how the guerrilla bands down here are set up. Naturally we'll scout ahead before leading our greenhorns over the ridge into quién sabe land. Meanwhile, this box canyon makes a good camp site for us to leave them forted up in. Help me drag these guys over to the stream. Some of the dames might have delicate feelings. But the current will carry them for miles before they start to stink."

It only took a few minutes to send the two dead rats bobbing off down the rio. It took a little longer to catch the spooked mules. But they managed, and rode back.

When they rejoined the others, Captain Gringo announced, "Numero uno, don't drink the water until those guides who led you into ambush float by. Shouldn't take 'em long now. Numero segundo, we're going to lead you up into the box canyon at the head of this valley, and you ought to be pretty safe there for now. Then Gaston and me are going to scout the way out of here."

Someone asked, "Don't you know the way out, Captain Gringo?"

Captain Gringo said, "Call me Dick. Do you really *want* to pop your heads over that ridge to the east without knowing if anyone's laying for you on the far side with a gun?"

That made sense, even to a greenhorn. So, having buried their dead, pissed in the bushes, or whatever, they all fell in to follow him as he took the point, with Gaston trailing behind to cover their rear, just in case.

Captain Gringo walked this time, having resaddled and returned the riding mule to one of the women. The little brunette Canadian girl, Pam, walked her own mule beside him. She was prettier than anything else ahead, and since they'd flushed the two outlaws in the canyon it seemed safe enough. But she kept pestering him with questions he either didn't want to answer or had no answer for. He lit a claro and spent a lot of time puffing in meditation as he answered her in monosyllables.

As the path swung near a bend in the stream, Pam gasped and said, "Oh, dear, is that a *body* I see there?"

Captain Gringo glanced at the white-clad peon, face down in the water with a damned boulder he'd snagged on keeping his corpse in place, and grunted as he said, "Yeah. Don't worry. He's way downstream from where you'll be getting your coffee water this evening, Miss Pam."

"Brrr, you make it sound so clinical. Tell me, what does it feel like to kill a man, Dick?"

"I didn't kill him. Gaston did. Oops, here comes his pal around the bend."

"Oh, my God, they both look so . . . so *dead*. You *were* the one who machine-gunned those others back there, weren't you?"

"I cannot tell a lie. I done it with my little Maxim. Is there any point to this discussion, Miss Pam?"

"I've just always wondered what it would feel like, if I had to kill somebody. How many people have you had to do it to, so far?"

He shrugged and replied, "Who counts? If you're asking if I get a kick out of it, the answer is no. It doesn't feel good, it doesn't feel bad. I know you're supposed to feel guilty about it. Maybe I would, if I had to murder somebody. But I'm a soldier of fortune, not a hired assassin. So it's never come up."

"I'm glad. That means it's not true what they say about you murdering a fellow officer back in the States, right?"

He took a thoughtful drag on his cigar before he said, "I killed the officer of the day, breaking out of an army guard-house. They were going to hang me in the morning and he came to gloat about it. I killed him and changed the plans Uncle Sam had for me. I guess you could call what I did murder. I know the U.S. Army does. It felt more like self-defense to me at the time. Since then I've killed other guys, because it was me or them. If that makes me an ogre in your eyes, go back and chat with less-exciting guys, Miss Pam."

She didn't take him up on it. She said, "My, you *are* bitter, aren't you? Why are you so bitter if it doesn't bother you to kill people?"

"Because the bastards keep trying to kill. *me*, of course. Like I said, I don't shoot at people because it's fun. I'm a very easy guy to get along with, if you don't point a gun at me. But there seems to be a lot of that going around, down this way."

She sighed and said, "So I just noticed. We were warned

in advance the people down here were all pretty nasty but..."

"You were told wrong," he cut in, adding, "Ninety-nine out of a hundred people down this way are just as decent as those you'd meet anywhere else. I like *most* Hispanics. It's that one out of a hundred you have to look out for. The problem down here isn't so much the culture as the law, or the lack of it. Leave a mess of poor downtrodden people to fend for themselves as best they can, and some are bound to wind up fending a little more than they really need to."

"But the other night in the market, when you had to save us from those awful greasers, Dick..."

"One reason I had to save you was that you were *acting* like you thought of them as greasers. The politer term for people down here of mixed blood is 'mestizo' in Mexico or 'ladino' in South America, with either term likely to be used in between. Blacks are called mulattoes whether they're part white or not, because they all say they are. The Creoles of pure Spanish blood are called Castilians, no matter where their ancestors came from, or simply blancos, meaning whites."

"A Spanish Creole is a *white?* In New Orleans they say..."

"You're not in New Orleans," he cut in, explaining, "French colonists picked 'Creole' up from the Spaniards and used it, wrong, as a polite word for people they otherwise looked down on. Since the breakup of the old Spanish empire, some pretty dark Latin Americans seem confused about the term, too. So it's better to avoid 'Creole' when you don't know the local meaning. But if a Hispanic calls himself a Creole, he's telling you he's from an old Spanish colonial family, see?"

She frowned and said, "It's all so confusing. But I'll try

not to call them anything if they don't call me a gringa. That's their insulting term for us, right?''

"Not really. They'd call you a *puta* if they really wanted to be nasty. Gringo or gringa doesn't mean anything at all in Spanish. Some say they got the term from the first American settlers in Texas when it was still part of Mexico. As the wagon trains rolled in, a lot of them were singing Protestant hymns for some reason. An old song called 'Green Grow the Lilacs' was a favorite that became the 'Battle Hymn of the Texas Republic.' The local Mexicans of course had no idea what a Green Grow could be, but it was easy to say.''

She laughed and said, "You're joshing me!''

He said, "You can look it up. Meanwhile, ride on up into that canyon ahead and we'll talk about it later. This is where I get off the train for a while.''

She looked confused. He pointed at a heel print in the mud by the rio and explained, "This is where those bandits forded the stream. So they must have come from the next valley east via that gap in the rimrocks over yonder. They didn't bring their mounts or adelitas, I mean girl friends. Lieutenant Verrier and I'd better check it out.''

She said to be careful and rode on. Captain Gringo stood by the side of the trail, directing others who approached in turn to follow Pam up into the box canyon and dig in. At last Gaston approached, leading their last mule and yakking in French with an Italian-Swiss and a Swede who didn't speak English. So Captain Gringo had him chase the Red Cross workers up the trail and told Gaston, "I'm going over that ridge to the east for a look-see. How do *you* feel about it?''

Gaston shrugged and said, "When one must go to the dentist, it is better to get it over with, hein? Hopefully they had a lookout posted up in that gap, and, even more hopefully, the adelitas and sissies ran away when they saw the Red Cross was not as helpless as they'd been led to feel. Otherwise, we shall of course be walking into an ambush.''

Captain Gringo nodded and unlashed the Maxim from the pack saddle again as he said, ''When you're right you're right. I'll take the lead. Can you handle that mule and a Winchester at the same time?''

''I'd rather not. But let's get it over with. My Italian-Swiss chum just told me they shall be serving French cuisine for supper this evening. So I want to get back in time.''

They waded across the thigh-deep stream and forged up the far slope with the heavy weapon riding Captain Gringo's left shoulder. The game trail the outlaws had used wasn't much more visible in real life than it had been on their map after being erased. But from time to time the big Yank in the lead spotted a boot-heel mark and, once, a broken match stem only someone lighting a smoke could have dropped.

Going through the obvious pass like a big-assed bird could have been injurious to one's health. So, near the top, Captain Gringo crabbed to one side on the now steep and treacherous slope to scramble up and flop behind a yucca clump for a peek over the crest.

The valley to the east was much higher and drier. It was little more than an arroyo just below the ridge itself. A campfire's ashy remains were still smoldering a hundred yards beyond the notch the bandits had used. There was nothing much else in sight. Captain Gringo stood up and signaled Gaston to move on up through the pass with the mule. Then he trudged down to the abandoned fire to see if he could cut any sign.

As Gaston and the mule joined him, he pointed at the confusion of hoof and human prints all around and said, ''They must not have liked noise. I make it thirty-odd ponies.

The adelitas got to ride, for a change, when their lookout ran down here to tell 'em things weren't going so hot. They took off to the south at full gallop. Would you say that means they're headed for the border?''

Gaston kicked an egg-sized object in the dust with his toe and said, ''Perhaps. I like *this* evidence better.''

''What is it? It looked like an acorn, but I've never seen an acorn half that big before.''

''I have. The live oaks in the highlands to the south grow to a très formidable size. They are too bitter for human consumption, of course, but horsemen in the high sierras carry them along as fodder for their mounts. Perhaps they are an acquired taste for mountain ponies, hein?''

Captain Gringo nodded and said, ''One and one makes two, then. They were in contact with treacherous guides from that coastal village to the west. But I'd say they're based in the border country. They probably spend more time as smugglers than bandits. A bandit could starve up here, waiting for anyone worth a full-time bandit's time.''

''Oui, had they not been a bit bush of the league, even you and me would have had a little more trouble with them on the other ridge. They should have had at least one man posted to guard their derrieres, non?''

''That's what I just said. The ridges running south-southeast look pretty rugged. We'd better scout the one we just came over as far as the rocks above the canyon we herded our flock into.''

Gaston shook his head and said, ''Mais non, why waste time? Had they been able to approach the canyon rim above the falls they would have set their adorable ambush up there instead of the more mundane slope we blew them down, non?''

Captain Gringo shook his head and said, ''We just agreed

they were half-assed bandits. Might have been lazy as well. I want to make *sure* there's no way a really determined guy couldn't work his way up above the falls. Before we settle down for that French cooking, I want to know nobody figures to drop a boulder in my soup!''

They moved back up to the craggy ridge and followed it as far as they could to the south-southeast. It soon became obvious that if the thugs lying for the Red Cross column had considered ambushing them in the canyon, they'd had a good enough reason for dropping the notion. The slopes on either side got steeper and steeper until the mule could go no farther on the razor back of broken basalt, and, while Captain Gringo thought he could probably work his way a *little* farther toward the canyon rim, he wasn't about to make it all the way without Alpine gear.

They turned back, led the mule as far as the game trail through the gap in the ridge, and made their way down and back across the stream to rejoin the Red Cross team.

Captain Gringo nodded approvingly when he saw how some of the men had formed a barricade of bales and boxes across the trail where it bottlenecked between two huge andesite boulders. He told them what they'd found on the other side of the ridge to the east and added, ''It's going to get hotter before it gets cooler. This canyon's about the coolest place to siesta within miles. I doubt anyone will hit us before three-thirty or four this afternoon. But a couple of you should keep an eye on things here anyway.''

One of them asked, in a Dutch accent, ''Then we'll be staying here tonight at least, ja?''

Captain Gringo shook his head and said, ''Just until moon-rise. You can't beat a moonlit night for traveling in Apache country, even when it's not Apache country.''

He led Gaston and the mule up the canyon to where the

rest of the party had spread out and mostly flopped around the pretty little pond at the base of the waterfall. He raised his voice to be heard as he called out, "Okay, gang. We've scouted some and you'll be glad to hear they can't get at us from those cliffs above us. But, as you see, the *sun* can. You'd better break out your tents and put up some shade. I want you to rest as much as you can until dark. So if any of you are up to sleeping, for God's sake sleep. Whoever's cooking, plan on a good solid meal before we leave here. But don't serve it any later than five. We'll be moving out around eight this evening and, sorry, ladies, but I have to say it's better to relieve your bowels in the bushes here before we hit the trail. That water should be safe, since it's coming out of mountains people can't get to for miles. I don't have to tell you to fill your canteens and water bags. Since some of you might not be used to arid country, I'd better tell you to drink as much water as you can this afternoon and then drink some more. We don't know how soon we'll be in such good shape for water. Water your mules well before we leave, if you have to shove their noses in it. Meanwhile, I see a couple still wearing their packs and tethered. You're not old cavalry troopers, so I won't cuss you out about that. Just get those damned mules unloaded and free to water and graze. Don't waste any oats on 'em here. There's plenty of grass and forbs. Any questions?"

The red-faced Englishman named Cecil raised a hand and said, "I have one, sir. You told us you know the way. Yet you just said you had no idea where the next water might be. Explain yourself, sir!"

There was a worried murmur from the others as Cecil's question sank in.

Captain Gringo raised a hand for silence and said, "We know the direction to the border and the grain or general lay of the ridges between here and there. You should have noticed by now that the water situation in these hills is a sometimes thing. Right now this waterfall is running pretty good. A few days from now this whole valley could be bone dry, while the dry valley we just scouted to the east could be in full flood. That's why I may lead you into the Valley of Death before I'll let you camp in a dry wash. Next question."

Cecil sniffed and said, "In other words, you two are just *guessing* at the best route to the disaster area."

Cecil was right, but Captain Gringo shook his head and said, "We were on our way there ourselves when we bailed you greenhorns out this morning. We're still headed that way, whether you want to follow us or not. Frankly, we don't give a damn. We could move faster on our own, and I think we just proved we can take care of ourselves up here. If you people would rather select another leader, do it now. Once I lead you out of here, I'll get testy as hell if anybody doesn't follow my orders on the trail."

Pam, the little brunette, sat straighter in the grass to call out, "This is no time to bicker amongst ourselves, dammit."

To Captain Gringo's surprise, the big dumb blonde, Trixie, backed her, saying, "Here here. Captain Gringo's already gotten *me,* for one, out of more than one sticky wicket! You're acting like an old woman, Cecil. You know perfectly well you couldn't lead a line of ducks across Regent's Park without getting lost!"

Cecil grumbled, "Maybe so. But I say, I'm not a perishing Yankee renegade!"

Before Captain Gringo could say anything, Gaston nudged him, stepped forward, and in a grotesque French-accented parody of an Oxbridge accent said, "I say, old bean, would you like to have a fight with a frog?"

Cecil blinked up at him, gasped, and said, "A fight, with *you*?"

Gaston said, "Oui, it would be très ridicule to expect you to fight this adorable moose avec moi. But I am smaller and older than you. So it should be fair, non?"

"Dash it all, Frenchy, I never said I wanted to engage in fisticuffs with *anyone!*"

"Non? Then why do you persist in speaking like a man looking for an argument? Are you just a silly species of, how you say, twit? Down *here*, mon ami, when a man is not looking for a fight, he keeps his lips from waving in the breeze, hein?"

Cecil looked as if he'd certainly like to crawl into a hole about now, if one were handy. Captain Gringo laughed easily and told Gaston to simmer down, adding, "We're all friends here, Gaston. I'm sure Cecil knows as well as you that we've all the enemies we really need in the surrounding hills."

Cecil nodded eagerly. So Gaston said he could always beat him up another time and led the mule away to unsaddle and graze it. Captain Gringo laid the machine gun on the grass near Pam and Trixie and sat down beside them as others moved closer to hear if he had any further words of wisdom. He didn't. He placed his sombrero upside down in the grass to hold the smaller parts as he proceeded to fieldstrip the machine gun. Pam was too smart to ask him why. But Trixie did. So he explained that after one had fired a gun it was a good idea to clean it.

Pam said, "Speaking of cleaning vital parts, I wish that pond were a bit more private. I haven't had a bath since we left the coast and that water certainly looks inviting!"

He laughed and said, "That's a good idea. We have to wait for moonrise before we leave this canyon. That means a good two hours and a change of total darkness. We'll let you nursing sisters take the first skinny-dip. Then us guys can slosh the grime off while you dry out, and we'll all start out squeaky clean.''

Trixie asked dubiously, ''What if someone peeks? None of us girls thought to bring bathing costumes, Dick.''

He removed the Maxim's bolt, wiped it with the oily rag he'd taken from a hip pocket, and set it aside with a silent shrug. Pam giggled and said, ''Pooh, what can anyone see in the dark? I'm already hot and sticky and it won't be dark for hours. You do as you please, Trixie. I, for one, mean to scrub my bod in that yummy pond as soon as I can. Do you think it's going to get any hotter before sundown, Dick?''

He unscrewed the recoil rod and said, ''Yes. If you girls are sharing a tent, you'd better put it up. Face the opening toward the cliff and you'll be able to siesta with your duds off.''

Trixie gasped and said, ''Really!'' but Pam laughed and said, ''That's a good idea. Actually, we each have our own pup tents. Poor Dr. Fitzke said they'd be cooler.''

He shrugged and said, ''Well, at least the mosquitoes have less room to dodge, in a pup. You of course brought plenty of mosquito netting?''

''No. Should we have?''

He grimaced, worked on a screw that wanted to argue with his jackknife, and, when it gave, said, ''I didn't think he'd been down here before. Have either of you ever had yellow jack?''

''Good heavens, no! Why do you ask, Dick?''

''You may get lucky. It's drier up here than in the low-lands. Won't have to worry about the bugs, much, when we're not camping near still water. But that Guatemalan disaster area we're headed for should have well water and irrigation ditches no matter how dry the country between the villages might be. I sure wish you people had mosquito nets. Gaston and me have already lived through yellow jack. So we're okay.''

Trixie asked, ''Do you believe that superstition about mosquitoes transmitting tropic fevers, Dick? Modern medical opinion dismisses it as an unproven native notion.''

''I don't know who's right or wrong. Vampire bats were a native superstition too, until some educated people got bitten by 'em down here. I do know that fevers, mosquitoes, and swamps seem to go together down this way. I've never seen yellow jack in dry country. I've seen a mess of it where it's wet. But let's not worry about it this afternoon. You won't meet many bugs in this particular canyon.''

They got up to go pitch their pup tents. Others around him who'd heard the conversation nodded and did the same. Gaston rejoined Captain Gringo, hauled off his boots, and sat closer to the water, soaking his feet as he said, ''Eh bien, the Spencers and their ammo have been issued to the troops and I am hungry. How is that adorable gun's digestion this lovely afternoon?''

''Not bad. That new smokeless powder doesn't gum the works up much. But it's more acid than black powder, so it evens out. Keeping the weapons in order could be a problem in the next big war, though. Even green troops can see a gun needs cleaning after it's fired black powder. But the noncoms are really going to have to ride herd on guys too lazy to worry about steel that still looks clean.''

Gaston lay back on his elbows, splashing his feet, and said, ''In that case I shall try to avoid the next big war. The little ones you keep dragging me through are quite enough. That is one of the things I am sitting in this hot sun with you to discuss in private, Dick. I have been discussing the situation ahead with some of these Red Cross types.''

''And?''

"It seems we have once again been handed a man's job for a boy's pay. The insurance company did not know, or neglected to inform us, that the first rescue team, who now seems to require rescue, managed to get several messages out before they were cut off in the disaster area. Disaster would seem to be an understatement of the situation in the Guatemalan highlands. *Holocaust* would have been the term I would have used. The first team reported themselves up to their adorable derrieres in volcanic ash and rotting corpses. Unfortunately, at least half of the natives they went in to help were still alive when they arrived. But dying like flies with très monotonous regularity even as they watched. Such food as they had to begin with, which is never much in a peon community to begin with, has been buried under tons of ash. In case you are wondering why they didn't simply dig it up, the ash would seem to be très poisonous. All sorts of amusing acids seem to go with fresh ashfalls from Boca Bruja, the adorable big-mouthed witch. They call her Boca Bruja because her vomit is cursed with a chemical brew their own white witches do not understand. Getting back to the first Red Cross team and the très fatigue nurse we were sent to rescue, I doubt we'll find any of them in condition to be anything but buried, if the volcano hasn't already done so. Their last runner made it out, just, by skirting a rapidly rising lake of boiling acid water."

"We already knew they were cut off by a dammed mountain stream."

"Oui, but did they tell us the main village up there lay in the tainted headwaters of that very stream, or that we are discussing the only source of drinking water for miles?"

"Oh boy. But by now they'll have moved to higher ground and drilled some wells."

"How? If the area was not a jumble of cliffs and canyons, nobody would need to be rescued. They would have simply moved themselves and the native survivors out of the disaster area, non? As to the drilling of wells, where would you suggest one drill a well in poisoned ash? La Boca Bruja coughs up a witch's brew of lava, ash, and steam. Said steam is laced with sulfuric acid, florine, lead arsenate, and other salts one would hardly wish to drink tequila with! Before you ask if the Red Cross team did not pack water in with them, they did. But hardly enough to last *themselves* this long, let alone desperate natives!''

Captain Gringo dropped a length of fishing line down the Maxim's disassembled barrel to pull an oily patch through it as he nodded and asked Gaston if there was any point to all this gloom and doom.

Gaston said, ''Oui. By now those adorable sluts who tried to betray us to los rurales will have gossiped about us back in town. So everyone should assume we are on our merry way toward the border. If we simply went back, changing our clothing discreetly and keeping out of the limelight until we could hop a coastal freighter . . .''

''You've been out in the sun too long,'' Captain Gringo cut in, adding, ''You're crossing your bridges before you come to them, too. We don't know what lies ahead of us. We know for sure that at least two dozen rurales and a couple of putas who know us on sight are laying for us back where we came from. Besides, I just told these other Red Cross people we'd get them through, some way.''

''Mais to *what*, you species of braggart? Nobody named that volcano Boca Bruja because of her lovely smile, and even if we can get to her, there is no way to go, afterwards, but back the same way! So why do you like to *walk* so much? Sooner or later, the only way out will be through that same disgusting little seaport, non?''

"Maybe. Meanwhile, the longer we stay away from it, the longer the law has to lose interest in us."

He started putting the gun back together as he added, "Go find some shade. That's what I'll be doing as soon as I finish here. I guess it's safe to leave the water jacket empty for now. On the other hand, I don't know when we'll ever see so much water again. Let me think about *important* matters for a change, dammit!"

Gaston sat up, called him a species of idiot, and picked up his boots to walk off barefoot through the grass. Captain Gringo finished reassembling the Maxim, decided it was safe enough where it was, and got up stiffly to look around for some shade, too.

There wasn't much. The sun was to the west now, but not as far as it would have been had it wanted to show any consideration. The few trees in the canyon were low and scrubby and their meager leaves didn't cast enough shade to matter. He saw that most of the Red Cross team had pitched pup tents and, smarter yet, mostly along the base of the now shaded cliff. They were half in shade and half in sunlight, since the afternoon sun cast a narrow ribbon of shade near the grassy base of the sheer rock wall. He nodded and legged it over that way. He got to the cliff and sat down in the grass with his back to the rock. The rock was still warm, but not as warm as it had been. By doubling his knees he could brace his heels in the sod with his feet in the shade as well, and the strip of shade would widen more in a while, so things could have been worse. He took off his hat again, wiped his face, and lit a claro. The sunlit pond and waterfall in the distance sure looked inviting. But ladies brought up under Queen Victoria's odd rules screamed so loud when they saw a naked man in public.

He couldn't imagine what in hell the dame screaming in the

nearest pup tent had to scream about. But she was screaming
pretty good. So he drew his .38 and rolled to his feet to run
over and find out.

As he dropped to his knees and opened the flap of the pup,
he saw Pam huddled against the far end, wide-eyed, yelling
for help, and brunette all over. She didn't have a stitch on.
She was staring not at him but at another visitor. A nasty-
looking but harmless vinegarroon was crawling across her
bedroll toward her as if it meant to crawl up her snatch or
worse.

Captain Gringo laughed, reached in, and grabbed the
vinegarroon, saying, ''Take it easy. You'll have the whole
camp here in a minute and it's too hot to get dressed.''

She gasped and said, ''Are you crazy? You can't pick up a
scorpion with your bare hand!''

He said, ''I know. It's not a scorpion. It only looks like one
to keep birds and pretty girls from eating it. They call it a
vinegarroon. They always seek shade in the heat of the day. It
wasn't out to hurt anybody.''

She heaved a sigh of relief, suddenly noticed what she was
wearing, and gasped as she said, ''Oh, I'm naked and you're
looking at me, you beast!''

He sighed, said, ''Come on, vinegarroon. Us beasts ain't
welcome here,'' and backed out, dropping the tent flap back
in place. He tossed away the harmless mock scorpion, put his
.38 back in its holster, and moved back to keep his sombrero
company some more. He'd dropped his smoke in the grass
when he'd heard Pam scream. So he picked it up and got it
going again just as a couple of other men moved toward him
along the cliff, guns in hand, to ask what was going on. He
grinned and said, ''False alarm. One of the nursing sisters
saw a big bug.''

They looked relieved and went back to their own shelters.

Captain Gringo enjoyed a few minutes' peace and quiet. Then Pam came out of her pup, bareheaded and barefooted, but wearing her blouse and skirt again, to come over and say she was sorry for calling him a beast.

He shrugged and said, "You had every right to feel upset. Forget it."

She didn't. She sat down beside him and said, with a becoming blush, "I'm not used to men popping in on me when I'm not wearing a stitch. Not lately, anyway. But it was still very silly of me. I mean, when a lady screams for help, someone is supposed to *come*, right?"

He smiled as he considered how nice it would be to come indeed for her, now that he'd seen what she had to offer under that prim uniform.

But he knew how she'd meant it and answered, "You weren't silly. You were scared, as you had every right to be. Vinegarroons are ugly little buggers and they do sort of look like scorpions."

"I thought it was going to sting me to death. Harmless or not, I'm glad you killed it."

He frowned and asked, "Why would I want to do that, Pam?"

"You didn't kill that ugly creature?"

"No. Just tossed it away. Vinegarroons can't help being ugly, to us, at least. It could have been a pretty girl, to a boy vinegarroon. I'm not sure how you can tell. Anyway, it's long gone by now."

She stared at him thoughtfully and said, "I just don't understand you at all, Dick. Just a few hours ago you mowed down a whole band of men, and yet you worry about the feelings of a *bug?*"

He took a drag on his claro and said, "You're right. You don't understand me. It's too hot to pontificate on the difference between harmless creatures and killers. Let's hope you never have to worry about it as much as I do.''

"At the rate we're going, I'm afraid I might! I understand the difference, Dick. I'm not *that* stupid. What I'm trying to understand is how you make your mind up so quickly. I mean you don't seem to hesitate a split second. You seem to be able to take a life or spare it, without taking time to *think!*''

He shrugged and said, "Killing's not a thinking man's game, Pam. I think pretty good when I'm playing chess or poker. But taking the time to ponder the best game plan can get you killed in a firefight.''

"You're so gentle. Yet you can strike like a cobra with no more feeling than a deadly reptile. I've never met a man like you before.''

"You've already said that more than once, Pam. Let's talk about the kinds of men you *have* met before. You said before that nobody's seen you naked *lately*. What are you, a reformed hoochie-coochie dancer?''

She giggled and said, "That's silly. I meant my husband, back in Canada.''

"Oh? I'm sorry to hear you're a widow, Pam.''

Her jaw clenched firmer as she said flatly, "I'm not. If you must know, I'm divorced.''

"I didn't say I must know anything. What happened back home is your own business. So don't tell me about it if you don't want me to hear about it.''

She must have wanted him to hear about. She spent the next twenty minutes or so telling him a very boring story. He knew the moment she said her ex-husband had had a drinking problem how the rest of it went. But Pam must have wanted to get it off her chest to someone who couldn't gossip about it in Canada. So he had to listen to all the dull details of a young wife trying over and over to straighten out a hopeless drunk until, in the end, she'd somehow wound up trying to save other lost causes for the International Red Cross. It could have been worse. The last dame who'd told him the same story had wound up an oversexed missionary and they were *really* no use to Spanish Catholics.

He knew he was supposed to render a value judgment as Pam wound down at last. Instead, he asked her if she wanted a drag on his cigar. She said she didn't smoke, and it was a little early to ask her about other vices she might have. She saw he wasn't about to tell her the story of his own life and finally said, "My, I do go on, don't I? All I really meant to say was that I'm really grateful for the way you helped me and, well, you're forgiven for peeping at me like that."

He grimaced and said, "I didn't peep, dammit. It was your idea to yell for help in your birthday suit."

"Don't be angry, Dick. I just said *I* wasn't, dammit! A lot of girls would be very cross with you for, ah, seeing so much of them."

"A lot of girls are dumb, then. This may come as a hell of a surprise to you, shorty, but in my day I've seen lots of naked ladies and more than one was built a lot better."

She blanched, called him a bastard, and flounced back to her tent.

He chuckled and took another drag on his cigar, trying to remember just when he'd seen a nicer little naked body. But, come to think of it, old Pam made the last two dames he'd seen that way look pretty sick. The insurance dames had been stacked pretty good. As good as Pam? It was hard to say. He'd have to get another look at Pam in some more interesting positions if he really wanted a fair comparison.

He told his cigar, "Don't talk dumb. We have enough to

worry about right now. Besides, we haven't seen any of these *other* dames naked, yet."

They ate at five. The food was the best Captain Gringo and Gaston had tasted in some time. The International Red Cross might not carry guns as a rule, but they traveled first class. After sunset the ten nursing sisters took a bare-ass dip in the pond in the dark, and, though their girlish giggles were more than a little stimulating to the glands, none of the men saw anything, dammit.

Later the other men joined Captain Gringo and Gaston in the water in turn. So they started out cool and clean. But by the time they'd loaded up and were on their way, the warm dry air had them all feeling as if the refreshing plunge had been but a childhood dream. At least none of them would stink for a while.

Captain Gringo left the machine gun lashed to his mule as he led them over the ridge to the higher valley. At night, automatic fire didn't offer such an edge, but dew condensing on old cold steel at night could play hell with the mechanism. So the Maxim was better off under its tarp for now.

As he'd timed it, the moon was just right for reading hoofprints in the dust as he led them south-southeast after the runaway survivors of the bandit gang. He'd turned the mule over to an otherwise useless unarmed Danish medic so that he and Gaston could scout ahead with their holstered pistols and ported Winchesters. From time to time Gaston insisted on pointing out a hoofprint Captain Gringo had already spotted. Gaston was like that. The moonlit road was clear and looked more well traveled than anything one figured to find on any official map. There wasn't much cover to worry about on either side of the smugglers' road, deer trail, or whatever the hell it was. When Gaston pointed out more sign, Captain Gringo said, "Dammit, Gaston, those adelitas left on ponies, not big birds. Of course they went this way. Where the hell else could they have gone?"

"Eh, bien, but when one goes *anywhere*, one has a *destination* in mind, and if we are marching on some bandit enclave . . ."

"There you go with your fucking bridges again. This trail leads toward Guatemala. We're trying to get to Guatemala. Maybe they are, too, if they came from there."

"But why? Would people with sense enough to run away from machine-gun fire be dumb enough to march on a very nasty volcano in full eruption?"

"I'll ask 'em when we catch up with 'em, if they're dumb enough to let us. Uh-oh, here's where life starts getting complicated."

Gaston said, "Oui, I warned you it was scabland," as they both stared down at the solid rock surface ahead of them. The old lava flow was flat and offered no hindrance to further progress, but it stretched flat and featureless as far as they could see in the moonlight. The man leading their mule caught up with them to ask what was going on. Captain Gringo said, "Keep us in sight and let the mule have his head on this slick rock." Then he started on as if he knew where he was going.

They marched across the flat lava for a little over three miles and saw a solid hedge of thorny chaparral ahead in the moonlight. Gaston said, "Merde alors. Know any *other* shortcuts, Dick?"

Captain Gringo dropped to one knee, felt the hard lava flow with his fingertips, and said, "Yeah, east. That's where this shit flowed from, so it has to lead to higher ground."

He led the long straggling column east along the south edge of the old flow for about another mile. Then, as they came to a gap in the chaparral and spotted the sandy trail leading south in the moonlight, he said, "As I was saying, guys running silver into Guatemala and guns into Mexico have to trend generally north and south."

He started down the new trail. He saw hoofprints going south and said, "I see 'em, Gaston. No, I don't know if we're talking about the same band. There must be lots of people in the smuggling business this close to the border."

"Oui, avec *guns*. Anyone could be covering this trail from the adorable brush on either side right now, too!"

"Stuff a sock in it. Who the hell could be waiting to ambush us around here, Gaston? We didn't know we were coming ourselves until just a few minutes ago. If this is the same trail at all, that dog-leg crossing the lava was a pretty neat way to get a stranger lost up here. I'm beginning to see why los rurales don't like to patrol this far south."

"I don't like it either, Dick! Los rurales are très tough! If they feel nervous about this country, that is good enough for me!"

Captain Gringo told him to shut up again and trudged on. The new trail ran fairly straight and was easy to follow, for about a mile. Then they came to a fork in the road. Captain Gringo cursed and stopped. Gaston said, "Me too. *Both* those trails can't lead to Guatemala."

"When you're right you're right. But don't tell the others we're lost just yet."

"It should not take them long to guess, if we don't choose one or the other, non?"

"I think it's time we called a trail break anyway. We'll let 'em piss and smoke here while each of us scouts ahead. You want the right or left fork, Gaston?"

"I hate them both. But I'll take the left. What difference does it make?"

"Probably not a hell of a lot. But who knows what may lie

around the bend or over the next hill, as the poets say? We'll
each scout a couple of miles, come back, and compare
notes.''

They stopped worrying about it as the others began to catch
up. Captain Gringo called out cheerfully, "Take ten or more,
and smoke if you got 'em. But no other fires, and go easy on
the canteen water for now. We're going ahead to scout for bad
guys.''

Someone of course had to ask why they had to scout both
roads, and Gaston snapped, "Merde alors, has it not sunk in
yet that these hills are très lousy avec bad guys? Enjoy your
break while you can, you species of idiot. We shall not give
you long here.''

Gaston strode out of sight up the left fork, cursing. Captain
Gringo laughed, told everyone he'd be back sooner or later,
and took the right fork.

He hadn't gone far when he began to wonder why. The
narrow trail was beginning to trend downhill now, and he
knew the Guatemalan high country had to be uphill, if they
were still in the foothills of the Sierra Madres. On the other
hand, mountain trails sometimes dipped down where they
didn't rise up. So he decided to give it a chance. He found
himself in a tunnel of mesquite as the already narrow trail
punched through higher ground on either side with the thorny
branches meeting overhead. They shaded the dust too well
even to look for sign. But when he stepped in horse shit he
knew someone had ridden this way recently, so he went on.

Over on the other fork, Gaston found himself moving
*up*hill in less brushy country. He instinctively hugged the
uphill side, and as he saw he was about to top a rise, he
dropped his smoke and crushed out the glowing tip with his
heel before moving on.

He went over the rise and beyond, then stopped, with a

dreadful Arabic curse, when he saw yet *another* fork ahead of him in the moonlight!

"By the multiple tits of the Pope's Protestant mistress, enough is enough!" he told himself as he stared morosely at his multiple choice. The fork to his left seemed less well traveled, but trended upward. The other ran straight the way he'd been going. He shook his head wearily and told his unseen comrade, softly, "If you want my considered opinion, Dick, we are, no shit of the bull, really lost!"

He started to turn back. Then the gray hairs on the back of his neck tingled as he heard the scrape of a hoof on stone. He moved into a clump of mesquite, as silently as a snake on tile, and hunkered down to cover the trail with his cocked Winchester.

A million years later a white-clad figure came down the trail to the left, leading an overloaded burro. Gaston watched until he saw the peon-costumed figure was alone, then stepped out on the trail to say politely, "Buenas noches, señor. Is it not late for you to be out alone?"

The man with the burro froze in place and gasped as he said, "In the name of Santa Maria, do not shoot me, por favor! I am only a poor old gatherer of firewood! I am not worth robbing, I swear!"

Gaston said, "One can see your burro is overloaded with dry sticks, viejo. But I seldom hold people up for firewood in a land so filled with it. Where you intend to sell it is no concern of mine. But let us discuss the distressing condition of the highways in this part of Mexico. If I wished to get to Guatemala from here, which way would you suggest I go?"

The old man shrugged and said, "In God's truth, I do not know, señor. The trail I just came down leads nowhere. I have never followed the other path, so quién sabe where it may or may not go, eh?"

"Merde alors, you are a big help, I must say. Let us begin with the trail you do know, since you just came down it."

The other man said, "It winds up into well-wooded country, as you can see from my load. I think perhaps Indios used this trail in the old days, since there are some Indio ruins up in the valley where it ends. Unfortunately, it leads nowhere else important."

"Eh bien, and you insist you have never followed this other trail to the right, viejo?"

The old man shrugged and said, "I have been down it perhaps a kilometer or more. But some cabrón has cut all the good firewood down that way. So I did not have any reason for to follow it further. It may go on to some important place. You can see it is wider and how the dust of many animals covers it. It must go somewhere important, no?"

Gaston said that sounded reasonable, thanked him for his modest directions, and stepped out of his way. The old man said he was glad to be of service and started to lead his burro on. Gaston shifted his Winchester to his left hand, reached up to draw the dagger from his neck sheath, and stabbed him in the back, twisting the blade inside to sever the aorta as well as the kidney under the victim's floating rib.

He left the knife in the body for now and grabbed the lead of the nervous burro as its master flopped face down in the dust with a sad little sigh. Gaston led the burro to a clump of brush and tethered it, saying, "Easy, mon petit. *You* were not the one who fibbed to me so outrageously, so you have nothing to fear, hein?"

He leaned his rifle by the side of the trail and moved back to recover his knife and wipe the blade clean on the seat of the dead man's white cotton pants and put it away before he searched the corpse. He found a bigger-bored derringer than one might expect a peon woodcutter to pack and put it in his own pocket, saying, "Shame on you. Ah, what a nice money belt. The price of firewood must have risen lately."

He dragged the dead man well off the trail by the boot heels, stood up, and said, "Eh bien. My regards to the carrion crows and ants, mon ami. If you will excuse me, I would like to see just what your sweet little burro is carrying under that camouflage of worthless sticks."

He went back to the burro, muttering, "Firewood indeed. More than a day's march from the nearest stove, in hills très lousy with such dry chaparral?"

He petted the burro, told it he loved it, and cut the cords to let the outer layer of brushwood fall away. The pack saddle under the camouflage was loaded with a substantial ammo box on either side. The moonlight was bright enough to read the stenciled letters, which said, in English, REMINGTON ARMS. BALL AMMUNITION, .30-.30.

Gaston chuckled and told the burro, "Just the size we need for our machine gun, mon petit! We are well met this evening, non? I knew the moment I regarded your lovely form in the moonlight that you were overloaded with something more than *firewood!* But let us rejoin the others and I shall relieve you of some of that load, hein?"

Meanwhile, on the other trail to the west, Captain Gringo had seen nothing so far and was about to turn back. But there seemed to be light at the end of the mesquite tunnel, and since it was too orange for moonlight, he decided he'd better check it out.

He moved cautiously out of the brushy cut, noting that the trail curved down and around into a flat-bottomed valley. The orange glow he'd noted was reflecting off the bare slope ahead. It was being cast by a burning shack below him, on the floor of the valley. There was a pole corral with no livestock in it. Three human figures were just visible, clear of the burning shack. Two of them were bending over a third on the ground. He heard a long keen of hopeless grief. The last time he'd heard a similar sound it had been an Apache squaw, keening over a brave who'd zigged when he should have zagged, going up against the old Tenth Cav. Gaston had *said* the Indians down here were, well, Indians. But the people down there were dressed Mexican peon. The one on the ground was the only one in pants.

He headed on down to see what all the keening was about, holding his Winchester down at his side politely. It still seemed to scare the shit out of them when they spotted him. One of the women leaped up and ran away. The other, holding the man's head, didn't.

When he got within earshot, Captain Gringo called out, "Don't be afraid. I won't hurt you."

The one holding the man's head sobbed and replied, "In the name of the Virgin, how much further *can* you hurt us, now? Why did you come back? You raped us both, you took everything we had, and my father is dying, you filthy ladrón!"

He came on in, saying, "You have me mixed up with someone else, señorita. I am called Ricardo Walker. I am not a ladrón. What happened here?"

The mestiza girl, for she was sixteen at the most, said, "See for yourself. They were not content for to shoot my father and rape both my mother and me. They torched our house after robbing us. Then they drove off all our stock. They even took our *chickens!*"

He nodded and knelt on the other side of the wounded peon to feel the side of his neck. He said, "He still lives. Where was he hit?"

"What difference does it make? Are you a doctor?"

"No, but have I got a nice surprise for *you!* First let's see if he's good for another half-hour or so. It's going to take me that long to get help for him."

"Do not hurt him," she warned, as he gently opened the bloody front of the wounded man's thin shirt. Captain Gringo whistled softly and said, "He's lung shot. But it could be worse. I'm traveling with a medical team. Are either of you women hurt?"

"They beat us and raped us many times. The women with them laughed while they were doing it. Why would men who already have women with them wish for to humiliate us like that, eh?"

"We've agreed they were bastards. I think I know the band. If it's any comfort to you, we've already shot about half of them."

"It is no comfort. It will be no comfort if you shoot *all* of them. We have both been raped. I was a virgin, until tonight, and now I may be carrying the child of a filthy ladrón!"

He said, "Take it easy. The nursing sisters may be able to do something about that, too. I can't do anything more here, now. But I'll be back in less than an hour with medical attention for all three of you. Try to keep your father quiet and don't try to move him. The less he moves, or breathes, the better. Understand?"

She shrugged and said, "Go with God, then. But my poor papa is still going to die, and I shall have to kill myself if I am pregnant by a damned ladrón!"

He got up and took off, jogging fifty and walking fifty in turn, and it still seemed to take forever to get back up the hill and along the trail to where he'd left the others.

He got there at last to find Gaston yakking with them about some damned burro. He shouted, "I need an emergency medical team on the double. Two raped and beaten women. A middle-aged man with a bullet in his chest and I think a collapsed right lung. I'm riding back on this mule, sidesaddle or not. The rest of you follow as best you can. But I'll be mad as hell if there's not at least one doctor with me as I dismount!"

He mounted one of the women's riding mules, sitting it right, even if it did mean riding with only one stirrup, and headed back. He heard trotting hoofbeats coming after him, looked back, saw at least two other riders close enough to matter, and heeled the mule into a lope. So it was only a few minutes before he, Pam, and the Italian-Swiss doctor who thought best on his feet reined in near the burning shack.

The older woman had come out of hiding now. She still looked scared as hell. The Italian-Swiss, whose name was Luigi, Pam said, dropped to his knees by the wounded man and opened his medical kit to go right to work. Pam asked if there was anything she could do to help. Captain Gringo said, "Both the women have been raped. What do you suggest?"

Pam took her own black bag from her saddle and, in not too great Spanish but a no-nonsense tone, said, "You two had better come with me. We won't want the boys watching what we have to do."

As she led them into the darkness, Captain Gringo asked Luigi what the wounded man's chances were. The Italian-Swiss said, "It depends on how healthy he was to begin with. A collapsed lung is not a matter to be taken lightly, even by a younger and stouter man. This poor specimen is undernourished, and from the color of his skin I would say he's had a bout of malaria or jaundice lately. Maybe both. The sanitation down here I've seen leaves much to be desired. Let me see, now. . . . Ah, here is the bullet, and thank God it did not break up when it went through the rib cage. Infection inside is in the hands of God. All I can do is clean the entrance wound and close it. His lung will reinflate in time if he lives that long. But how are these people to keep from starving to death first? You say the bandits took all they had?"

"Yeah, they didn't even leave 'em a chicken. How soon will it be safe to move that guy, doc?"

"He's hardly going to get much bed rest *here*. Are you thinking of taking him along with us, captain?"

"Got to. You just said we can't leave them here without a bite to eat. The people in Guatemala need us too. What happens if we rig up a litter for him between two burros?"

"It can't hurt him worse than leaving him behind. But it's not what I'd order for a patient anywhere at all civilized. The odds are fifty-fifty he'll die on the trail. I suppose that's better than the certain death of leaving him behind."

Captain Gringo couldn't argue about that. Others were coming into view now. Gaston had mounted up to lead the way, on a little burro he was riding bareback. As he joined Captain Gringo he said, "Meet Pepito. He used to belong to a gunrunner who overloaded him shamefully. The .30-30 rounds I relieved Pepito of are coming aboard larger and stronger mules, hein?"

"Would you run that by me again, Gaston? What was that about a gunrunner?"

Gaston said, "I encountered a dear old man who lied like a rug. Do not worry about him anymore. He's no longer with us. The point is that the lying bastard informed me the trail I met him on did not lead to Guatemala. Ergo, it must lead to Guatemala. He never picked up brand-new Yanqui ammunition on *this* side of the border. That is not how the game is played. Mexico has guarded seaports and an oppressive government but plenty of silver. Guatemala has a more relaxed customs service but is very poor, so. . . ."

"I only asked what time it was, not how to build the clock!" Captain Gringo cut in with a laugh.

He saw the Italian-Swiss doctor consulting with some other medics on how best to sling the wounded peon between two beasts of burden, while Pam was returning from the darkness with the subdued but relieved-looking peon women. He nodded and asked in English how she'd made out. Before Pam could answer, the young girl dropped to her knees in front of Captain Gringo and took his hand to kiss it. He said, "Oh, hell," and Pam said, "Her name's Fabiola. I told her you were our leader. They both seem pleased with my, ah, standard first-aid in such cases. The mother here is going to have a real shiner by morning. But they're both in pretty good shape now."

He helped Fabiola to her feet and told her they were taking the three of them along to Guatemala. Her mother keened some more and the peon girl explained that they didn't want to go to Guatemala.

He asked, in that case, where they *did* want to go. Fabiola said, "We have friends and relations higher in the hills, señor. We are not supposed to discuss family business with strangers, but you are not strangers, you are lifesavers. If we can but make it up to some old Indian ruins our friends and relations sometimes use for to hide from los rurales . . ."

Gaston had been listening, bemused. He asked, "Would any of these relatives of yours include a man about my size and a little older, who, ah, cuts firewood on occasion?"

Fabiola replied, "That sounds like Tío Hernan. Do you know him, señor?"

"We ah, traded burros earlier this evening, I believe. He said something about not wanting someone to recognize his burro, wherever he was going with his, ah, firewood."

She nodded and said, "That sounds like Tío Hernan. He has always been the clever one in the family business."

Captain Gringo just looked at Gaston, who looked back innocently and said in English, "How was I to know? She just *said* he was a liar."

Gaston was too polite to point when the column passed the spot where he'd left the dead smuggler. He simply dropped back with a shovel and made sure no buzzards, or relatives, would find the remains by the dawn's early light after all.

Since he still had the dead man's burro to ride, it was easy enough for Gaston to catch up and rejoin an expedition forced to move no faster than its slowest pedestrian could walk. As he moved up to fall in beside Captain Gringo in the lead, Gaston didn't mention what he'd just been up to. Little Fabiola and her mother were in earshot, leading the burros her wounded father's litter was slung between.

Captain Gringo didn't have to be told what Gaston had done. He had the natives near the head of the column both to verify the way and hopefully to keep their friends and relations from opening up on the Red Cross expedition on sight. It was clearer now what the wounded peon and his womenfolk had been grazing back at their out-of-the-way rancho. The bandits who'd shot them up had known about the fresh horses in their corral, too.

The moon was low and they'd covered lots of ground despite trail breaks when Fabiola showed that she'd recovered enough to think clearly once more. She called out, "Let me run ahead and tell our people who is coming and for why, Captain Gringo. They are not used to meeting strangers so high in these hills. It might be better if you all waited here until I return, eh?"

Captain Gringo nodded and called out, "Trail break, but no smoking and keep spread out." Then he told Fabiola to go ahead. As the girl jogged out of sight up the trail, he saw the Italian-Swiss doctor and a Dutch medical opinion move in for another look at her wounded father. So he moved back to his own pack mule and unlashed the machine gun. He left it atop the saddle to be polite, but had it armed and handy just in case.

Pam and Trixie joined him as he draped the tarp, loosely folded, over the water jacket and let the ammo belt dangle. Pam asked if he thought there'd be any need for machine-gun fire and Trixie asked how he was making out with the pretty little greaser. He grimaced and said, "You keep talking like that and I probably *will* need to use a gun on her people, Trixie."

Pam said, "She's a *mestiza*, right, Dick?"

He shook his head and said, "For the record, I'd say nearly pure Indian. Probably a distant relative of the ancient Maya. This was Maya country, once. But they won't mind if we mistake them for Spanish."

Pam said she'd try to remember that and asked if there was anything they could do to help. He said, "Yeah, move back down the trail and give me a clear field of fire up it."

Pam said, "Oh, he's bitter again," in a hurt voice and led Trixie away, bless her.

Gaston came over, leading his stolen burro, to ask what *he* could do to help. Captain Gringo said, "You might have gotten rid of that burro by now, you asshole. These people *don't* think every burro looks alike."

Gaston shook his head and said, "Mais non, that would be even more suspicious, Dick. I introduced Pepito to them just in case they *had* recognized him back there. Leave it to me should anyone ask for a bill of sale. You know how well I can shit the bull, hein?"

"You may be right. But for God's sake watch your step. Fabiola's friends and relations are only one step removed from out-and-out bandits themselves!"

"Oui, that is why I took out Tío Hernan. Had I let him move on to meet the rest of these greenhorns, he might not have met them. He might have gone back for assistance in relieving them of their goodies. To these Indio hillmen, our boots alone represent a fortune, hein?''

"Okay. You probably did the right thing. What do you want, a kiss on both cheeks and a medal from me?''

Gaston laughed and said, "I'll settle for that big blonde, Trixie. I can see you have the inside track with the petite brunette.''

"Don't talk dirty. Don't mess with that dumb blonde, either. She's trouble with a big fat T!''

"Merde alors, *all* women are trouble with a species of T. But what else is there to fuck that is not disgusting and probably just as much trouble? I don't think any of the men with us are mariposo, anyway, and the female mules are a little too big, even for me.''

Captain Gringo laughed at the picture but warned, "Stay out of that blonde anyway. If Fabiola can get us an Indian guide, we're as good as there, and I don't want any lovesick Red Cross dames slowing us down once we grab and run.''

"Can I make nice-nice with the overinsured M'mselle Swann, if you don't want her? She'll doubtless be easier to convince, once *one* of us has seduced her, non?''

"For chrissake, don't you ever think of anything else, Gaston? For all we know the dame's a dog. Nobody told us what she looks like.''

"True, but who *cares* what she looks like? She has to be prettier than my fist. I am getting hard up again, since those adorable treacherous bitches ran away.''

Captain Gringo suggested he go into the bushes for a while and, spotting the Italian-Swiss passing, called him over to ask what was up. Luigi said, "Actually, I'm on the way to take a piss. We think the wounded peon will live if the village his daughter mentioned is not too far from here.''

"Can we afford to leave him in their care, doc?''

Luigi shrugged and said, "He'd be far better off in a hospital, of course. But if infection doesn't set in, bed rest and a lot of warm soup will do as much for him as we can, dragging him along. Dr. Kruger and I were just discussing it. Kruger agrees it's better to risk leaving him behind as the lesser of more than one evil. We still have many more patients to worry about up ahead, and . . ."

Captain Gringo cut in to say he understood, and Luigi went to take his leak. Captain Gringo stepped into the nearest clump of chaparral to do the same while he had the time. Pissing was no problem. But it was sort of annoying to do so with a semierection. He wondered why he had one. He'd had more than enough sex with Pilar and Concepción the night before, and nobody around here seemed to be offering. So he told it to behave and put it back in his pants.

He moved back to the machine gun fast when he heard voices, a lot of voices, coming down the trail toward them. Some of the voices sounded like they wanted to argue.

Fabiola and a male chorus of bigger and tougher-looking natives joined him as Gaston drifted closer, Winchester lowered politely.

Young Fabiola introduced everyone. For some reason, all the Mexican Indians seemed to be her uncles. The one doing most of the bitching was Tío José. He said, "We mean no disrespect. The girl has told us what you people did for her own. But strangers are not welcome on our land."

Captain Gringo smiled thinly and replied, *"Your* land? Funny, on the map it says these uninhabited hills belong to *Mexico."*

Tío José spat and said, "I piss on the map. I piss on the grave of El Presidente's whore of a mother, too!"

Captain Gringo laughed easily and said, "Great minds run in the same channels. We don't like dictators either. Has

Fabiola explained we're only passing through on our way to Guatemala?''

"She has. You can't go there by way of the trail we used to travel. It crosses the border near Boca Bruja, and the volcano has devastated everything for kilometers around.''

Another tío said, "Es verdad. Our amigo Hernan just came from there with the last, ah, firewood. He said he was afraid he would not make it, as Boca Bruja rained cinders on him and his burro. When he topped a rise and looked back, near the border, everything in his wake was covered with smoldering ash.''

Tío José stared thoughtfully at Gaston and said, "Speaking of Hernan's burro. How is it this girl says you have it now? I do not wish for to call any man a liar, but I find it most strange that Hernan would trade beasts with a total stranger, señor!''

Gaston shrugged and said, "I found it strange too. But what could I do? He was pointing a derringer at me.''

One of the other tíos chuckled and said that sure sounded like old Hernan. But Tío José said, "Not to me. Hernan was a most cautious man. He lived to be very old by stealth, not gunplay. There is something most peculiar going on here!''

Gaston snorted in disgust and said, "Eh bien, if you must know, I stabbed your friend and robbed him of his burro. Then, having nothing better to do, I joined my friends in rescuing his relatives here. You know how idiotic we Frenchmen are, hein?''

It worked. Tío José still grumbled. But when Fabiola's mother came over and wailed at them to cut the bullshit and get her man to safety, they grudgingly turned to lead the expedition on. As they did so, one of them warned Captain Gringo to consider it a one-way trip and that all bets were off if they ever spotted strangers on their smugglers' trail again.

The tall American assured them he had no idea how he'd ever be able to point it out on any map in any case. They told him not to try.

It wasn't a village they led the expedition to. A side trail a casual passerby would have had trouble spotting led up to what looked at first like an outcropping of jumbled black rock but turned out to be on closer inspection a complex Maya ruin, overgrown with cactus and chaparral. The semipermanent smugglers' camp was set up in what had once been some sort of ceremonial courtyard. The substantial campfire in the center was invisible from any distance but illuminated the facade of Maya glyphs and gods all around. The Indians had erected brush lean-tos along the walls, and naturally a mess of women and children boiled out to giggle and point as the Red Cross column marched in. The tíos told them to move back and behave themselves as the wounded man was carried into one of the shelters with his worried wife and daughter. One of the tíos told Captain Gringo they could corral their mules and burros in another courtyard with their own stock and that they were welcome to use the fire, but that the smugglers had no food to spare. Captain Gringo said that was only just, but asked if they could hang around until daybreak. His informant nodded and said, "You will break your necks if you try to follow the trail south after moonset, señor. As you shall see, it runs along the sides of sheer cliffs in places."

"Could one of you guide us, if we paid well?"

"No. Do not press your luck with us, señor. We are desperate people leading desperate lives. We would have had to kill you, had you come this far as total strangers. But we owe you for the lives of three of our friends. So you are free to go in peace. But that is all we owe you. Besides, even if one of us wished for to go on with you to the border, the border is not there anymore. Everything is covered with hot

ash and lava down that way. We are, how you say, out of
business until Boca Bruja goes back to sleep for a while.''

Captain Gringo agreed to the terms of the smugglers'
rough-and-ready hospitality, directed his followers to corral
their stock and share some coffee with the somewhat surly
band, and hunkered down to eat, himself, as both the unre-
constructed Maya and their ancient gods frowned down at him
from every side. He ate because he didn't know when he'd
get another crack at a warm meal, not because he was really
hungry. The situation was still a little tense. But by the time
some of the Indians had joined them around the fire to accept
coffee and smokes, he figured it was going to be okay. He'd
seldom met an Indian anywhere who didn't consider smoking
with a stranger a friendly act. Some of the nursing sisters
helped even more by breaking out some chocolate for the
kids.

But Captain Gringo wasn't about to go to sleep in such
unfamiliar surroundings, and in any case the night was more
than half shot. So as things settled down he got up and went
for a walk alone. Nobody seemed interested in following him
as he left the firelit courtyard and mounted the slope of what
had once been an imposing flight of steps. At the top, he
found himself on an elevated ceremonial platform of some
kind. It was pretty dark up here, now that the moon had set,
and the blocky weathered statues of forgotten Maya gods and
godesses all around looked sort of spooky. But not as spooky
as the glow he spotted on the southeast horizon.

He moved across to a waist-high parapet and leaned on the
weathered blocks for a better look. The skyline down that
way was etched black against the orange sky glow. He didn't
see anything that looked like a volcanic cone. So the peak of
Boca Bruja itself was still far to the south. But from the way
it was illuminating the sky above it, the volcano was still

erupting pretty good. That smuggler Gaston had knifed had said the ash was falling as far north as the border, and the disaster area was said to be almost a full day's march beyond!

He heard a soft footstep and turned to see a dimly visible white-clad figure approaching. It was little Fabiola. She said, "I saw you going up here. I wished for to be alone with you. We have not had time to speak alone together, señor."

"Call me Dick, Fabiola. What's on your mind?"

She joined him at the parapet, looking down as she murmured, "I do not know much about talking to men, Señor Deek."

"Is there anything I can do for you? Are you feeling better now?"

"Sí, much better, but confused. That nurse was most simpático about what happened to me. She did things for to keep me from having a baby and told me how to do things for myself until such time as I might wish one. You Anglos are so wise about such matters."

"I wish we were as wise as you about your country. You, ah, wouldn't want to show us the way south, would you?"

"Alas, I do not know the trail, even if my people would let me. We shall never see each other again, after this night ends, Señor Deek."

"That's what I thought. So what else are we talking about, Fabiola?"

She wiped her nose and said, "That most simpático nurse told me many things about men and women as she treated me. She was very wise. When I told her I had never lain with an hombre before those men ravaged me, she said she understood how I felt and why it was natural for me to be most confused."

"I understand. As a woman who'd once been married, old Pam would be up on such girl talk. But I'm not a girl, Fabiola. So what do you want from me?"

"I want for you to fuck me, I think."

He laughed incredulously and asked, "Did Señorita Pam put you up to that?"

"No." Fabiola sighed. "She just told me it was only natural that, toward the end, as the last and most gentle bandit did bad things to me, I was not sure about my feeling when he . . . stopped."

Captain Gringo nodded and said, "I see. Our bodies are like that, I guess. But don't you think it's a little early to find out if you were, ah, missing something?"

"Señorita Pam asked me if I knew what an orgasm was. She was so simpático I could not lie to her. I confessed how even a virgin's natural curiosity can lead her to sin, with her hand and things. She said she thought the best way for to get over my confused feelings about that one handsome bandit would be to do it some more, with someone I liked better."

"That makes sense. Sort of. I never would have thought old Pam held such advanced views, though. But I'm afraid you came to the wrong guy, niña. Don't you have an Indio boyfriend who'd be willing to help you out with your, ah, problem?"

"Sí, many of our young men have serenaded me in the past, before my papacito chased them away. But you are very pretty, and I wish for to thank you properly as well, Señor Deek. Can we fuck now? Nobody ever comes up here this late at night."

He laughed gently and said, "Thanks, but no thanks, Fabiola. No offense, but I don't think it would be a good idea."

"Don't you think I'm pretty?"

"Very pretty. And very confused. I know a little bit about the way a woman's head works, too, and I'm afraid we'd both regret it in the cold gray dawn. I'm leaving at sunrise.

You're just too young and, well, confused, for a one-night stand with a passing stranger.''

She sobbed as she said, ''Oh, I hate you! You think I am not worthy of you because I am an Indian!''

''Querida, I want you so bad I can taste it. But someday you'll thank me for passing on your generous offer.''

She didn't thank him. She called him a stuck-up gringo son of a bitch and turned to flounce away, sobbing. He sighed and muttered to himself, aloud, ''Now why in the hell did I do that?''

A nearby feminine voice replied in English, ''Perhaps because you're a gentleman after all?''

He blinked in surprise and almost went for his gun as he whirled, spotted a more rounded ''statue'' sitting nearby with her back against a rose in the parapet, and asked, ''Is that you, Pam? I thought you were a gargoyle or something.''

She chuckled and said, ''I know. I beat you up here and I don't know why I didn't say something before I saw you had company and decided to just keep quiet.''

''I'm sure glad the two of you didn't make a sap out of me, then. Did Fabiola know you were so sneaky?''

''No. I never expected her to take my motherly advice so literally, so soon. You were right, you know. A love-'em-and-leave-'em quickie was not what I prescribed for such a young rape victim.''

He moved closer, saw she was sitting with her knees up and barefooted under her whipcord skirt and asked casually, ''Have you ever prescribed anything like that for *older* women, Pam?''

She shrugged and said, ''I didn't really enjoy the rather wild fling I had after my divorce. It got me through some otherwise lonely nights. But I'm a Red Cross girl now, so *down*, boy!''

"Aren't you being a little presumptuous, Pam? I generally get to make a pass before the lady says no."

"Don't make one, then, and I won't have to say no. I know what they say about gay divorcees, but I've outgrown that nonsense."

He didn't answer. So she said, "Naturally, you don't believe me. You think I'm a tease, right?"

He shrugged and said, "Let's not worry about it. I just turned down something younger and prettier."

"Why, you insulting unwashed gun thug!" she said with a gasp, as he turned away, having seen the light in every way up here. He made it halfway across the platform before Pam called after him, "Come back here, damn you!"

He shrugged again, returned to her, and asked her what the hell she wanted. She sighed and said, "I give up. Aren't you even going to *try*, you brute?"

He laughed dryly, took her in his arms, and kissed her, leaning her back against the weathered but smooth basalt. She kissed back passionately until he ran a hand up under her whipcords and discovered to his mild surprise that she wasn't wearing anything under her skirts. But as he parted her pubic thatch with his exploring fingers Pam stiffened and said, "No! I don't want to go that far!"

He kissed her some more and began to rock the man in the boat as she struggled weakly and tried to cross her naked thighs, as she sobbed and said, "Dammit, I don't want to be raped, you animal!"

He said, "Sure you do," and rolled her over on her belly with her breasts and everything else at that end hanging over the sheer drop into darkness as she spread her knees against the inside of the parapet to brace herself from going over the side head first, gasping in fear. So all he had to do was unbutton his fly, hoist her skirts, and shove it in, deep and hard, before she knew what was happening.

Pam moaned and said, "Oh, Jesus, you *are* raping me!"

He said, "I sure am. How do you like it so far!"

She giggled and asked, "Well, aren't you even going to *move* it, you terrible man?" So he did, and in no time at all they were old friends. He assured her he really thought she had a nicer ass than Fabiola, and she admitted that getting laid in such an odd position was a totally new experience for her. But after they'd come together that way and he hauled her back to do it right, she protested that lying down on solid rock was a bit much. So he leaned her against a flat-faced Maya god and wall-jobbed her, standing up. That was a new position for even a gay divorcee, too. She was so short that he had to hook an elbow under each of Pam's knees to brace her shapely little rear high enough against the carved stone, and she said it felt like a washboard rubbing her fanny as she clung to him, returning his thrusts with interesting gyrations she'd obviously practiced before. She'd been going without sex far longer than he had, so she found it easy to climax in any position and complimented him on his ingenuity. But she added, after climaxing again in such an odd one, that she really thought they should do it in her pup tent in the future. He said, "We'll be pushing on at daybreak, so this is the last chance we'll get for a while, doll box."

So she said, "Oh, in that case push me up a little higher so you can push it to me good."

They left as the eastern sky was just pearling gray, and it was broad daylight by the time the trail south started getting complicated. This was just as well, since the trail led over

razor-backed sierras and along some ravines not even a
Spanish mule would have wanted to meet in the dark.
Nobody in the expedition had gotten much rest the night
before. So when they found themselves high in a saddle
cooled by the trades, Captain Gringo ordered a siesta break
and they all caught a few hours' sleep. All but Captain
Gringo and Pam did, at any rate. She'd been right about it
being much nicer with their clothes off in her tent.

Gaston got into Trixie's tent, and Trixie, at the next camp
site. Other couples had made similar arrangements by this
time, if they hadn't before. But most of the men and at least
three or four of the girls were starting to look a little jealous
around the campfires. So Captain Gringo pushed hard for the
border to get rid of his greenhorns before someone started a
fight.

It was hard to say just where the border was. But they must
have crossed it somewhere as the hills around them got grayer
and grimmer by the mile. The trail was covered with what
now looked and drifted like cigar ashes. But when anyone
inhaled it, it tasted and felt like ground glass. It helped if one
tied a bandana across one's nose and mouth. So they began to
look more like train robbers than a relief expedition as they
forged south and, once over a pass, saw the slopes of Boca
Bruja looming ahead.

There was no mistaking Boca Bruja for anything else. The
volcano was a big gray bastard with a wide crater that made it
look more like a distant butte than a peak. The slopes were
eroded into a pleated skirt of deeply cut ravines. A dirty gray
mushroom cloud of steam and ash rose impossibly high above
the mountain, illuminated from time to time by flashes of hell
fire from the seething caldron below.

As they worked their way closer, the trail vanished completely
under drifting dunes of gritty ash with an occasional blackened

something sticking out of it. Most of the charred remains they passed were of course burned cactus or chaparral. Some of them weren't. Dead livestock was bad enough. One of the charred women had a well-baked baby under her when the Italian-Swiss and Dutch doctors were dumb enough to turn her over. After that they just walked past the charred bodies. There was nothing a medic could do for them now.

As they were working up an ashy slope, closer to the volcano, Gaston joined Captain Gringo in the lead and said, "This is senseless as well as très fatigué, Dick. We are not going to find anyone alive ahead."

Captain Gringo said, "We can't go back. Besides, the wind seems to be from the southwest. So the ashfall might be worse this way. If the first team's holed up in the lee of some ridge, they could still be breathing."

"Merde alors, breathing *what?* It stinks like rotten eggs and kitchen matches this far from that species of volcano, and you want to get *closer?*"

"Don't want to. Have to. It doesn't matter if we find Miss Swann alive or not, now. The only way out is by way of Guatemala, and that fucking mess ahead is between us and the lowlands. So pick 'em up and lay 'em down. The sooner we get past Boca Bruja, the sooner we'll be enjoying a cool drink in some nice steamship lounge."

"That's the first good suggestion I've heard in some time from you. What about these others? How long are we to be saddled with such greenhorns, Dick?"

"Depends on them, I guess. Are you tired of Trixie already?"

"Mais non, she uses that big mouth of hers most delightfully in the dark. But last night she said they meant to stay here until the emergency is over."

"They figure to be here some time, then. Look at that volcano go!"

Boca Bruja was clearing her throat now, with a roar that could be heard for miles. House-sized, white-hot boulders were flying up like chimney sparks to arc away from the main plume and bounce down the gray slopes, trailing cinders and smoke. Gaston sighed and asked, "May I be excused for the rest of the afternoon? All in all, I think I'd rather associate with bandits and rurales."

Captain Gringo told him to shut up and struggled to the crest of the slope. Then he paused, nodded, and said, "We made it."

Gaston joined him to ask, "Made what?" as they both stared down into the next valley. A village was spread out below. What was left of it anyway. The walls rising above the ash were flamingo pink, with pastel blue doors and window shutters. It would have been a pretty little highland village, had not the tile roofs been covered with a foot or more of gray ash, or had said ash not risen almost as high as the window sills between the houses. Here and there a tree rose, leafless, in a land where trees didn't drop their leaves if they felt at all well. As others struggled up to join them, Captain Gringo said, "Welcome to the last days of Pompeii. If that volcano doesn't shut up soon, there'll be nothing but a stretch of gritty-gritty down there in a day or so!"

Luigi asked if he thought there was a chance anyone was still alive down there. Captain Gringo said they weren't going to find out unless they went down for a look. So they started down.

They'd only gotten a third of the way down when people came out of the half-buried houses, yelling a lot. Pam shouted, "I see Red Cross uniforms! We got here in time!"

Gaston grunted and said, "In time for what?" but everyone else acted cheerful as hell, considering. The villagers and members of the cut-off first team helped them get the supplies down to the old Spanish mission, now serving as a hospital and supply camp. The nave wasn't very big. But there weren't a hell of a lot of survivors and the relief expedition hadn't brought a hell of a lot of supplies, so it tended to even out.

Captain Gringo let everyone sort things out and settle down a bit before he took a dusty doctor from the first team aside and asked which of his nursing sisters might be Cynthia Swann. The Red Cross man sighed and said, "Poor Cynthia's dead, I'm afraid."

"You're no more afraid about it than *I* am, doc! What happened to her?"

"Yellow jack. She and seven others in our party came down with it, and four, including poor Cindy, didn't pull through. I'd show you her grave, if I could find it now. But it's under tons of drifting ash. She and the others were buried in the village graveyard. We don't have one of those things anymore. As they drop, we just have to bury them wherever the ash is still soft enough. It tends to set like cement after a few days. Moist, you know."

Captain Gringo shrugged and said, "That's that, then. How do you go about getting *out* of here, doc?"

"You don't. I thought you knew we were cut off. The road we took in is covered by water that's acid enough to eat you alive. It seems to be going down a bit now. Probably leaking under the lava dam down the valley. But at the rate it's sinking, we'll be stuck here at least another few weeks. I hope you people brought enough food to last us and the villagers that long."

"How many mouths are we talking about feeding, doc?"

"Four hundred and forty-eight, assuming the last fever victims recover. Why?"

"We didn't bring enough food. A week's rations at most. We're going to have to get everyone out."

"But the road is blocked and . . ."

"Yeah, yeah, I know about the sluggish sewer drains, doc. But I just brought a mess of people in where the map said there was no road."

"Good! You can lead us all out that way, right?"

"Wrong. Aside from bandits, there's no telling what los rurales would do to a mess of Guatemalans too poor to bribe them. There's got to be another way. What happens if we just sort of ease around that volcano, low on the slopes? We're not that far from the west coast and it should be mostly downhill, past Boca Bruja."

The doctor shook his head and said, "We can't. We're cut off that way, too."

"By what, lava?"

"Worse. Bandits. A guerrilla band led by some idiot in a white hat has taken up positions in the next valley over. So far our alcalde and our military escort have kept them from raiding us through the one pass. But they say they won't let us through unless we give them a hundred thousand dollars, U.S., and we just don't have it!"

Captain Gringo grimaced and said, "They'd double-cross you once they had it, if you did. The ghouls want the women and supplies we have between us as well."

"That's what the alcalde says. He says medical supplies are worth their weight in gold to any rebel force and . . ."

"I just said that," Captain Gringo cut in, turning away to see where Gaston might be. He didn't see Gaston. A tall redheaded woman who was either about forty or very very tired had been listening to their conversation. As she came over, the Red Cross man introduced her as a Mrs. Parkhurst and added that she was not with his expedition. The redhead said to call her Ruth and added, "I'm a geologist, or the widow of one at any rate. My late husband and I were up here studying the volcano when it started teaching us some tricks that are not in the books. I couldn't help noticing you seem to have a machine gun on your mule, Captain Walker."

He nodded and said, "Yeah, but it won't work, if those bandits are dug in behind a razor back. I'm sorry to hear about your husband, though. What happened?"

She pointed at the church wall, albeit really in the direction of the volcanic slope to the west, and said, "Boca Bruja happened. I told him it was time to get out of there. But he thought he knew better. We were camped in the crater. He said he was sure it was extinct."

Captain Gringo whistled softly and said, "You sure must run pretty good, Miss Ruth!"

She smiled wanly and said, "I do. But not that good. Actually we had a tiff the night before the volcano blew. So I was staying here in the village when it happened. Hopefully, the first explosion killed him and our workers before they knew what hit them. I've been stuck here ever since. I certainly would like to get out of here."

"That sounds reasonable. Any ideas, Miss Ruth?"

"One. It may seem a little wild. If you're interested, I'd be glad to show you my plan on the map in my quarters."

He nodded and she led him out of the mission and up the street through ankle-deep loose ash with a yard of solidified crud under it.

Ruth Parkhurst's rented rooms were on the second story of the village posada. It was just as well. The cantina below had gone out of business after the ash drifting in had covered everything with what looked like gray cement. The roof beams above bowed ominously, and as he glanced thoughtfully at them she said, "I know. Some of the less substantial roofs have already caved in. Sit down. I'll get the map. I'd offer you refreshments if I could. But I can't. We're rationed one canteen and three tortillas a day. I hate tortillas. Don't you?"

He sat at the table in the center of the room and said, "They're okay if you have something to go with 'em. Living on tortillas alone can get to be like eating old blotters."

"You *have* been down here awhile," she said, as she spread a very well detailed topographical map on the table before him. She put a once-manicured and now grimy nail to the map, saying, "This is where we are, of course. The lake of acid water doesn't show, since it's not supposed to be there. But it's about here and, as you can see, blocks the only practical way out. The bandits are holding this valley to the south. As you see, there's only one easy way over into it, and they have it guarded by at least a dozen riflemen. So it's one of your typical Mexican standoffs."

He nodded and traced the valley they were in west until it turned into a ravine running up the slope of the volcano. All the other local drainage seemed to work the same way. He asked, "What if we just worked up to about here, moved along the side of the mountain well above the bandits, and took this other ravine down behind them to *this* valley?"

"You can't. At the moment it's full of lava. The flow is slow but sure. Lava moves like that, when a wind blows steadily across it to cool the crust. But at the rate it's going, in no more than a day or so it will have filled the valley beyond the bandits. Then *they'll* be cut off too."

"Ouch! Once Caballero Blanco figures there's no way out but through us, he's bound to try a little harder, right?"

"Exactly. I told the alcalde that, but apparently Mexican men don't listen to women, either."

"I think they're Guatemalan. But I get the picture. *I'm* listening to you, Miss Ruth. What's your plan?"

"Heavens, can't you *see* it? If we were simply to divert that lava flow into the valley the *bandits* are holding, they'd have two choices, and they'd have to make their minds up fast!"

"If I was Caballero Blanco I'd rather run like hell to the southwest than through a lot of rifle fire, too. But how do you go about diverting a lava flow, Miss Ruth?"

"I've got dynamite. Need I say more?"

"I wish you would. I'm a soldier of fortune, not a geologist, and you just told me Boca Bruja eats geologists for breakfast!"

She put her finger in a spot two-thirds of the way up the cone and said, "If we dynamited this knife-edged ridge, right here, the lava might find it easier going down this ravine instead of the other, since it's sheltered from the cooling effects of the prevailing wind, see?"

"Not really. You're talking about blowing a hole in the side of the flow way the hell above its moving front."

"Exactly. Where the lava is thousands of degrees hotter and a lot more fluid, Dick. The cooler foot of the flow is moving, but it's also acting as a dam ahead of the hotter and more fluid flow from above. Break a new conduit out for it, and it should spurt like puss and flow like the devil!"

"Oh, swell. And we're supposed to stand in front of it like big birds without wings?"

"Don't be silly. We'll light a very very long fuse and be well up the far slope before it blows, see?"

He fished out a cigar to give himself time to think it over as he studied her map. She asked if he could spare a cigar and he said, "Sorry. Wasn't expecting to meet a lady who smoked cigars so soon. Here. Let me light it for you."

He did and she inhaled as if it were a cigarette as she sat beside him, sighing as she said, "God, that tastes marvelous. I haven't had a smoke for weeks. My damned husband had all the tobacco with him up in the crater."

He didn't comment on her unusual views on widowhood. The map was more important. Like most West Point graduates, Captain Gringo had a good grasp of terrain, and even Washington had known you were supposed to take the high ground. He said, "Now I can see why those bandits didn't just work up and over. It won't work. The ridge between us and Caballero Blanco stays razorback, all the way to the top."

She nodded and said, "It's a basalt dike. Sheer-walled and slippery black rock, where the mountain filled a crack with lava ages ago and then let the rains erode it into a sort of Chinese Wall. So what?"

"So how do you get through it to cross the head of the bandit-held valley to your pet lava flow?"

"Easy. I told you I was here before the mountain went crazy. So I got to explore some on my own." She stabbed the map with her nail and said, "The bandits don't know it. My husband didn't even know it. But one day as I was picking flowers I found a lava tube running under and through the dike."

"You were picking *flowers* up there?"

"The mountain and surrounding countryside are quite pretty, between eruptions. Give the new ash a couple of years to weather and the villagers will actually have more fertile milpas to plant."

"Swell. But meanwhile we have to keep 'em alive that

long. Okay. You're on. I'll carry the machine gun and some of the dynamite. How much can you carry?''

"Enough. But are you talking about leaving right now?''

"Why not? Let's get out of here before your roof caves in!''

Captain Gringo said Gaston couldn't come along and told him to get over to the alcalde and his boys with as many guns as he could get to follow him. Then Captain Gringo followed Ruth Parkhurst up the side of Boca Bruja. For a lady packing thirty pounds of high explosives, wearing an ankle-length cotton smock, she moved pretty good. As he struggled after her with the Maxim on one shoulder, extra ammo belts around his hips, and another case of dynamite under one arm, he complimented her on her likeness to a mountain goat. She said her late husband had commented, not as nicely, on her restless nature. Captain Gringo could see how it might have been tough concentrating on geology and old Ruth at the same time. Aside from being tall and apparently tireless, she filled out that smock pretty nicely. The sun was high and as it shone down through her thin cotton skirts at him he couldn't help noticing how muscular the redhead's long legs were.

She suddenly crabbed sideways across the dusty gray slope and led him into the mouth of what looked like a railroad tunnel blasted through the wall of basalt columns otherwise blocking their further progress. She put down her own load in the welcome shade inside and said, ''We'd better rest a moment, if you're tired.''

"I'm not tired. I'm anxious to see if this works.''

"I'm glad you're as strong as you look. It has to work. But

I wish we had more dynamite. Why did you insist on dragging along that heavy weapon, Dick?''

''I'm not dragging it. I'm carrying it. To get the rest of the way we have to expose ourselves to the bandits in the valley below. I don't like to do that, even when I'm packing a machine gun. But what the hell.''

She laughed, picked her own load up from the sandy floor of the lava tube, and they went on. It wasn't easy, and the ravine between them and the lava flow was steep and slippery. Worse, they heard a distant shout and, looking down, saw someone below in a white hat and once white charro outfit, pointing up at them and yelling a lot. Captain Gringo said, ''Keep moving. We're out of range.''

The bandits didn't know this, or perhaps they just liked noise. For guns started popping down below and gouts of dust flew from the sides of their ravine, fortunately far too short to worry about.

Ruth dropped to her knees and began picking away at the wall of solidified ash in front of her with a geologist's hammer. He offered to help and she said she knew best. So he sat on a dynamite case with the Maxim across his knees and let her. Down below, the bandits couldn't have known what they were up to. But whatever it was, Caballero Blanco must not have approved. A skirmish line was moving upslope at them, blazing away and cursing at impossible range. As Captain Gringo watched bullets hit far down the slope, he grimaced and muttered, ''Stupid bastards.''

But it got less sillier as the sombreros down the slope kept moving closer, perhaps encouraged by the lack of return fire. Captain Gringo had found in other similar situations that people down here who had guns tended to fire them a lot. The guy in the big white sombrero yelled, loud enough to be heard all the way up the mountain, ''What are you waiting for, estupidos? Anyone can see they have no guns, and one of them is a *woman!*''

Ruth chopped away a big chunk and asked, ''Did he mean that the way I think he meant that, Dick?''

Captain Gringo said, ''Yeah. How's it coming?''

''Hot, dammit. The lava on the other side can't be far now. I can't dig much deeper without burning myself. Help me charge and pack this hole, will you?''

''Can't. I'm going to have to open fire in a minute if they don't wise up.''

She looked downslope, gasped as she saw how close the bandits were now, and broke open her first dynamite box, asking, ''Why don't you *shoot*, dammit?''

''You do your tricks and I'll do mine. I could probably hit 'em with plunging fire now, but we're still out of their range. So why waste good ammo?''

She charged the hole with her own dynamite and told him to move his big ass so she could get at the other. So, as long as he was standing up anyway, Captain Gringo braced the Maxim on his hip and opened fire down the slope.

The results were gratifying. When a guy got hit with a machine-gun round on a steep dusty slope, he seemed to roll forever, ass over teakettle like he was on fire. He sent the skirmish line back down to Caballero Blanco with his compliments. But when he tried to lay some lead on the white-clad bandit leader in person, the son of a bitch was just out of range and getting more out of range by the frantic leap.

As he ceased fire, Ruth was cursing like a sailor getting tattooed with a rusty can opener. He thought she was unsettled by the noise of gunfire and said it couldn't be helped. She snapped, ''Fuck the gunfire! How am I to detonate this fucking dynamite now?''

''Jesus, didn't you bring fuses and caps?''

"Of course I brought fuses and caps, God damn this country and its acid rain! The stupid caps are corroded green as an Irishman's shamrock and this fucking fuse is moldy, too!"

He said, "Okay. Run back up to that lava tube and hit the dirt. Be with you in a minute, I hope."

"I can light the fuses as well as you, dammit. I just don't know if they'll burn, or if the caps are any good if they do!"

He snapped, "Do as you're told and do it *now!* Don't argue with me, woman. Move your ass!"

She gasped and said, "That's not fair! I'm not packing a gun!" But then she saw something in his eyes that made her decide to move away, and once old Ruth moved, she moved good.

Captain Gringo looked down the slope, saw nobody moving down there, and reloaded his Maxim. Then he moved back to about pistol-fighting range with the muzzle trained on the unpacked hole filled with dynamite and fired a whole belt's worth into it. Or almost. He still had a couple of rounds left when a lucky round hit a lucky cap and the whole mess exploded in his face, knocking him on his ass to roll down the steep slope!

He spread his arms and legs to stop himself and caught the Maxim as it almost slid past him. He staggered back to his feet, ears ringing so hard he couldn't make out what Ruth was yelling about from the lava tube above. He moved up the slope to see that it had almost worked. A big black bubble of what looked like steaming tar was oozing out of the big hole he'd blasted. But he could see it was too crusted really to flow. He reloaded with the last belt, leveled the muzzle on the big boil of lava, and lanced it with another full burst.

Then he was running as if his life depended on it, because it obviously did. With the scabby crust blown away, white-hot lava was shooting out of the hole like the devil's firehose, and this was no time to hang on to an empty machine gun. He dropped it and scrambled up the slope toward the lava tube as the ravine he was vacating filled with a sloshing flash flood of newer liquid lava. It picked up his abandoned machine gun, exploded the ammo still belted to it like a string of firecrackers, and carried it down the mountain glowing white hot as Captain Gringo made it to the entrance, turned, and saw he'd just missed getting his boot heels burned off. The whole ravine was filled with lava as liquid as molten steel and moving down into the bandit-held valley at express-train speed!

Below, they could hear the distant crackle of small arms, and Ruth asked if the bandits really thought they could stop a lava flow with guns. He shook his head and said, "No. The ones trapped on Gaston's side are trying to get over the ridge in a hurry. That's not an easy thing to do, with Gaston manning the fireline. Uh-oh, I see a white hat on a white horse, and, talk about dumb, he's trying to run down the valley away from the flow!"

"There's no way out farther down. The valley's blocked by that same acid lake!"

"That's what I just said. Let's move back to the other side of this dike. It's getting sort of hot in here."

She said, "I know," and wrapped her arms around him to kiss him, with considerable appetite. He kissed back. Any man would have. But when they came up for air, he said, "You sure pick a funny time and place for romance, honey."

She said, "I haven't had enough romance to matter since I married a damned geologist. Do we really have to go right back down to the village, Dick? You know they'll want to talk and talk about what we just did, and it won't be dark for hours, outside."

He grinned, carried her deeper into the tunnel, and lowered her to the sand. As he'd expected, she wasn't wearing anything under her thin smock, and they used that under her to keep her back from getting gritty as he shucked his own clothes and mounted her. She wrapped her long muscular legs around his waist and sobbed as she said, ''Oh, Jesus, I've been wanting *that* big cigar since you offered me the other one a million years ago! I'm never going to let you stop unless you promise to take me out with you!''

He suggested they come before they go anywhere, and she thought that was a great idea. By the time he'd climaxed in her twice he would have promised to take her anywhere. She was younger and prettier than he'd thought, under the dusty clothes and hair. So he wanted to try her at least once in a bed after they'd both had a bath. She said that was a swell idea, too, and said she was looking forward to taking a shower with him. They rested in each other's arms, shared a smoke, and tore off another piece before she agreed, reluctantly, that they really ought to have a look at the current situation.

They dressed and moved out the other side of the lava tube. As they moved down the slope hand in hand, he stared beyond the village at the pea-green lake in the distance and said, ''Hey, I can't be sure, but from the yellow rim around the edges that wasn't there before, I'd say that lake is sinking, doll.''

She shielded her eyes, gazed thoughtfully, and said, ''From the steam clouds down that way, I'd say hot lava's hit water by now, and you know what they say about underwater shock waves. That yellow rim is exposed sulfur oxide. You're right, the lake's draining faster now.''

As they got down near the village, others rushed up to meet them, demanding to know what they'd done, since they'd obviously done *something* marvelous. Captain Gringo let

Ruth explain to the others as he spotted Gaston in the crowd and joined him to ask how the firefight had gone.

Gaston spat and replied, ''What firefight? It was like shooting fish in a barrel. Lava did most amusing things to the ones we rolled all the way down the slope into it. That lava was your notion, of course?''

''Tell you how we did it, later. Ruth's coming with us to the capital. I know Trixie and the other Red Cross girls will have to stay here to clean up. But you might find a Guatemalan girl who'd like to see the sea, right?''

Gaston's traveling companion was a mulatta named Lola. As Captain Gringo had assumed, both Red Cross teams meant to take more time getting the sicker villagers in shape to move. Dr. Luigi gave them a message to deliver, asking for more food and medical supplies, now that the trail to the lowlands was open again. Some of the Guatemalan soldiers who'd been cut off up there, and who, according to Gaston, had helped do a pretty good job of El Caballero Blanco's band, offered to go with them. Captain Gringo told them they'd better stick around, just in case any of the bandits had gotten away, or new ones showed up, attracted by carrion.

So in the end the two soldiers of fortune and the two girls left with the pack burro Gaston had acquired so dishonestly. Once they'd worked past the still slippery and acid slopes of the drained lake, the trip was more pleasure than work. As he'd expected, Ruth was even better-looking after they'd showered together under a jungle waterfall. She tried to tell him the story of her life as they spent the next few days, and nights, together. But he knew all he really needed to know about her and she didn't really want to hear all the details of his wild career, either, as they made love wildly every time they could get out of sight of Gaston and Lola, who probably had other things to talk about.

Ruth said it seemed all too soon when they came at last to the outskirts of Guatemala City. But by the time they got her to the cable office she was already walking a bit more primly and answering his cruder suggestions about hotels with thoughtful faraway looks. So when they got to the cable office, he held out his hand and said, "Well, I'll see you around the campus, doll. Thanks for the lovely evening."

"You *do* understand, Dick?"

"What's to understand? You gotta go back to the States and play respected widow of a distinguished scientist, right?"

"I'm afraid so, dear. What are you going to do now?"

"Duck a lot, I guess. Come on, Gaston. What happened to the burro and Lola?"

Gaston shrugged and said, "The last I saw them, they were going down an alley somewhere. One assumes she did not want to come all the way to the sea with us after all, hein? Don't worry, I knew better than to let her steal anything we still might have need for. We have our money and guns and, once in such civilized surroundings, what else does one need?"

Captain Gringo said he wanted to talk about money with other people. So they left Ruth at the cable office and legged it over to the hotel Gaston had already told him about along the trail.

It was the best hotel in town and, naturally, where insurance agents and other rich folk were likely to stay. They'd already changed back into their linens, which, if rumpled, were good enough to check in with, if they paid in advance. But nothing happened until later that night.

They were seated in the tap room, nursing their drinks,

when a large, florid fat man in a panama suit came to join them. He handed Captain Gringo a business card and said, "Heard you were in town. How did you boys make out? Is Miss Swann with you?"

Captain Gringo read the card, shook his head, and said, "No. She died before we could get to her, Mr., ah, Smith."

Smith, if that was his name, heaved a long weary sigh and said, "Shit, there goes the ball game, then. I guess we can't fault you if she was killed before you even got there. But the company's still going to miss the overinsured little bitch!"

He started to rise. Captain Gringo said, "Sit down, Mr. Smith. We're not finished yet. You owe us some money."

The insurance troubleshooter sat back down, but said, "I'm afraid you're laboring under some misapprehension, Captain Gringo. You boys *got* your front money. We can write that off. But one could hardly expect my company to offer you another dime for failing to carry out your mission!"

Captain Gringo took out a folded paper he'd been working on along the trail and said, "We didn't fail you. We went exactly where you sent us, and it wasn't easy."

"Of course you did. But if the client we sent you to rescue was dead before you got there, you can hardly expect us to pay you for rescuing her, dammit!"

"We want half. If you'll read this prepared statement, you'll see we pulled half your chestnuts out of the fire, at least."

Smith unfolded the paper and asked, "What's this? I can hardly make it out."

"So it's written in pencil on soggy map paper. It'll still hold up in court, once I sign and notarize it for you. The pencil's indelible. Borrowed it off a lady who draws maps a lot."

Smith read the prepared statement, frowning at first, then

breaking into a grin as he said, "By God, that's right! The double indemnity *was* for *violent death!* But isn't yellow jack a pretty violent way to go?"

"I'd rather be shot. But she still died of *natural causes*. Gaston here will sign it too. If we see a checkbook poco tiempo."

"But you two are notorious outlaws and . . ."

"You know that won't come up in any Chicago court," Captain Gringo cut in, adding, "I'll sign my name Smith, too, and Gaston here can be Jones if you like. The point is that once you can present that, notarized by Guatemala . . ."

Smith said, "You got it," and took out his checkbook.

They all parted friends at the notary public's office down the street when Smith took off to wire the good news. When the two soldiers of fortune were free to talk again, Gaston laughed like a mean little kid and said, "You know, of course, he could have gotten a death certificate free from the International Red Cross?"

Captain Gringo patted the breast pocket he'd put his check in and asked, "What can I tell you? I paid for my education. Let them pay for theirs. Which way's the railroad station, Gaston?"

"That way. But what is the great rush, my young and headstrong? We have booked two adorable rooms for the night, and the paseo in the plaza is about to begin. Have I failed to mention that the girls of Guatemala are très attractive, or that they are, how you say, nuts about handsome strangers?"

Captain Gringo laughed and said, "No, but why don't we go find out if you're right or not?"

The Best of Adventure
by RAMSEY THORNE

"THE KING OF THE WESTERN NOVEL" IS *MAX BRAND*